AUTHOR NOTE

This series is strictly fiction. Actual bureaus of meteorology do not work like this in real life. The author is very aware.

There has been creative licence taken in regards to weather tracking, prediction systems, and any/all meteorological practices mentioned herein.

It's just a fun and crazy ride intended for entertainment purposes only.

Enjoy!

OUTRUN THE RAIN

THE STORM BOYS SERIES
BOOK 1

N.R. WALKER

COPYRIGHT

Cover Art: Paper & Sage
Editor: Boho Edits
Publisher: BlueHeart Press
Outrun the Rain © 2023 N.R. Walker
Storm Boys Series © 2023 N.R. Walker

BLURB

Tully Larson has loved tropical storms since he was a kid and spent his summers with his dad in the wilds of Kakadu National Park. He's happiest outdoors, a rough and ready kind of guy who loves the power of Mother Nature and chasing the thrill of electrical storms every chance he gets.

Jeremiah Overton, a fulminologist from Melbourne, chases storms for a whole different reason. Lightning has shaped his entire life and he's driven to study it, to understand it, so heading to Kakadu in the middle of the storm season is a logical thing to do. After all, the Top End is the lightning capital of Australia.

Tully wasn't sure how a week at his remote *bunker* with an academic type would pan out. And Jeremiah didn't expect much from the storm-chasing cowboy who volunteered to take him.

But both men know all too well that when opposites attract, lightning strikes.

OUTRUN THE RAIN

N.R. WALKER

THE STORM BOYS
SERIES – BOOK ONE

CHAPTER ONE
TULLY

I SAT IN MY OLD JEEP WRANGLER, WAITING FOR THE plane from Darwin to come in. Jabiru Airport was no more than a one-building low-key airport, smack bang right in the middle of Kakadu National Park in the Top End of the Northern Territory.

It wasn't a thriving metropolis, lemme put it that way.

The brick terminal building was better than the tin shed it used to be, but still. Heathrow, this place was not.

Jabiru itself had a grand population of around one thousand people. Well, that many in the dry season, less in the wet season. The climate up here did funny things to folks, and most packed up and went south for a few months, before the heat and humidity and torrential rain set in.

That was when I got here.

Because with that heat and humidity came summer storms. Brutal, fierce, electrical storms that rolled in almost every afternoon, dumping monsoonal downpours, and setting the skies on fire with lightning.

Which was why I was waiting at Jabiru Airport.

A guy was coming up from the Bureau of Meteorology in Melbourne. Staying for a week or two to study lightning. Well, he'd already studied it; he had some doctorate or some other fancy title. Well, he had *Atmospheric Sciences and Meteorology* after his name, followed by a whole bunch of letters. He was coming all this way to *observe* it. To run some fancy tests, or some scholarly thing I didn't understand.

Apparently, he'd put some feelers out in the Darwin scholarly meteorology circles about wanting to spend a week in the wilds of Kakadu National Park studying and observing all he could. I was surprised he didn't get laughed at, but someone mentioned me—a non-scholarly type who spent weeks chasing electrical storms—and a few phone calls later, he'd tracked me down.

I'd told him I wasn't like those university dicks. I just spent my summers chasing storms because it was fun and because I could. I explained it involved camping out in Kakadu National Park. That there was some hiking involved. That it would just be me and him in the middle of nowhere, and there would be a possibility that we saw no other human beings for his entire stay.

He said that was fine.

He'd offered me some ridiculous payment, some government study grant, and I told him to donate it to the Kakadu National Park. He did exactly that, and I was all out of excuses.

So, despite my best efforts to convince him otherwise, he was getting in today.

Doctor Jeremiah Overton.

With that name, he had to be eighty. I'd not spoken to him on the phone, only via email with his fancy doctorate signature, but even the way he wrote was very formal. Or maybe that was just the way super smart scientists wrote requests from their fancy science websites.

I had no clue.

But I was about to find out.

The small plane flew in, went careening down the runway, and with a sigh, I climbed out of my Jeep and went inside. At least the terminal was air conditioned.

"Afternoon, Tully," Yasmin said from behind the check-in counter.

I gave her a smile. "Afternoon."

"What brings you in today? A person or cargo this time?"

"A person."

A person who I didn't know at all. Hell, I didn't even know what they looked like, didn't know what kind of time I was in for. *Why had I agreed to this?*

Regret ratcheted up a notch or two as the plane rolled to a stop and the door opened.

I had a bad feeling about this.

Me and some snobby old guy stuck out in the middle of the most remote scrublands, surrounded by deadly wildlife that he probably ain't ever seen before, while we chased electrical storms so he could probably stand out in the middle of a clearing holding a metal rod up to the sky . . .

I mean, what could possibly go wrong?

People climbed down the steps onto the tarmac and began to filter inside. Some of them already fanning their shirt collars against the heat and they hadn't even been here a minute.

I counted twelve people, about all that'd fit on that size plane. Some couples, which I scanned right past. A young mum with a kid on her hip. Definitely not. Two guys in suits, who I gave a hard pass. A young guy, who looked sexy in a nerdy kinda way, with his proper button-down shirt all tucked in and his navy shorts with hiking boots. *Nope, can't be him.*

Then I spotted a man. Seventy at least, wild and wiry grey hair under a bucket hat, dressed like Doctor Livingston from Jumanji or whatever fucking movie that was. He was the Jeremiah-ist looking man of the lot. So I made a beeline for him, grinned my fakest grin, and held out my hand.

"Tully Larson."

He looked at me, then at my hand, then back to my face and put his hand to his ear. "Whadya say, son? Gotta speak up. I'm deaf as a post."

Oh great.

I opened my mouth and took a deep breath so I could yell, just as the sexy shorts guy with his pretty button-down shirt and hiking boots interrupted me. "Tully Larson?" he asked. Christ, his eyes were like dark sapphires on steroids. So freaking blue.

"Ah, yeah?"

He held out his hand. "Doctor Jeremiah Overton."

Well, I'll be fucking damned.

"Some people call me Jeremy."

I grinned at him—my next week was now looking a whole lot brighter—and shook his hand. "Hey, Jeremiah. It's real nice to meetcha."

CHAPTER TWO

JEREMIAH

JABIRU AIRPORT WAS A DIRT STRIP IN A DUST BOWL. The heat was suffocating, and getting off the plane and walking into the humidity was like having a hot bath, only somehow the water was dry.

Welcome to the Top End.

I wasn't sure what to think of my guide, if that's what I could call him. Tully Larson's reputation preceded him. The team at Darwin University had said he was a wild card. He had no meteorological academic credentials but had earned himself a reputation as a smart and savvy storm chaser.

A storm chaser.

He might have reported his findings and taken some readings and footage a few times for local weather channels and the bureau here, but he spent weeks at a time on the front line of monsoon storms for fun.

For *fun*.

He was handsome, no two ways about it. Undoubtedly well and truly out of my league. He looked like a surfer from the Sunshine Coast in Queensland, with his longish blond wavy hair, but after hearing him speak, it was clear he was very much a Territorian. He had a laid-back manner to the way he walked and the way he talked. He had a drawl and an easy smile that made him instantly likeable.

My first impression of him was that he was an easy-going, smiling type, and nothing fazed him. Including monsoonal electrical storms. Nothing seemed to be a problem.

Although calling me by my shortened name seemed somewhat difficult for him.

"So, Jeremiah," he said, lifting my heavy equipment crate into the back of his Jeep. He lifted it effortlessly, then relieved me of my duffle bag as well, sliding it in beside my crate. "How was your flight?"

"It was fine," I replied, getting into the front passenger seat, and looked up at the scorching sky. "Does your car not have a roof? A canopy, perhaps?"

The sun was blisteringly hot, the humidity making it worse. I went to put on my seatbelt and almost branded myself with the buckle. "Ow!"

Tully laughed. "Yeah, sorry about that. And yeah, there's a canopy somewhere. But it's cooler without it once we get goin'. You'll see."

That was hard to imagine.

"So, I thought we could swing past the store and grab some last-minute supplies. We won't be back this way for a while."

"Sure."

I didn't know what *supplies* we could get that wouldn't

spoil in these hot and humid conditions, especially whilst camping. I was certainly too scared to ask. But he did this all the time apparently, so I'd need to trust him.

The store itself was more of a convenience outlet, with very few selections and exorbitant prices. "Wow," I mumbled, looking at the price of butter.

He smirked, slow and easy. "The prices? These aren't Melbourne prices. These are two-hours-from-a-super-market prices out here."

He grabbed things like bottled water, flour and sugar, canned goods, beef jerky, and dried fruits and nuts. And a jumbo roll of toilet paper. "The most important essential." He chuckled at my embarrassment. "Would you rather I didn't get it?"

"Uh, no, it's fine. Thank you."

He snorted. "Now, when were you wormed last? If we're gonna eat wild pig . . ."

I stared at him. Horrified. "Uhhh, I'll eat beans. And grass, if I have to, before I eat worm-infested feral pig."

He burst out laughing. "I'm just messin' with ya." He pushed the trolley, then stopped and looked back at me, very serious. "There was one time I did eat goanna. And brolga is tough eating." He made a face. "Like eating a rubber pigeon."

He laughed at my expression. "Just kiddin'. About the brolga. I totally ate goanna once."

I added a few more cans of beans to the cart and ignored the way he laughed all the way to the checkout.

"Afternoon, Tully," the man behind the counter said. He was about fifty with greying hair, sun-weathered skin, and a tired smile. "You headin' out again?"

"Yeah, mate. Got company this time," he said, nodding to me. "But I'll be sure to keep an eye on this one and make sure he comes back. Not like the last one . . ." I stared at him again, wondering what on earth I'd got myself into, and he laughed again. "I'm kidding!"

I looked at the man behind the counter. "You don't happen to sell a sense of humour, do you? I think I'm going to need an upgrade."

He rumbled a laugh. "Don't let him fool ya," he said to me. "Tully here knows what he's doing, so you be sure to listen to him, ya hear? Unless you don't wanna come back, that is."

Tully grinned at me and handed over his credit card, then we loaded the gear into the back of his Jeep. He looked up at the darkening sky and pulled the canvas cover over the food and my gear, but the front seats were still without protection.

I almost branded myself with the seat buckle again, earning another smirk from Tully. I was already beginning to rethink my first impression of his smile. At first, I'd thought it made him likeable. Now I thought it made him insufferable.

Cute, but incredibly annoying.

Or was it annoying me because I thought it made him cute?

I sighed and pretended not to care.

With his annoying smile firmly in place, he reversed out of his parking spot without so much as a glance behind us, then sped out of the small town of Jabiru along the Arnhem Highway.

The wind whipped around us, and he was right. The

air movement with the roof off did make it more bearable. The humidity was thick with the threat of rain, even though the sun still beat down on us. The passing scenery was spectacular—sub-tropical greenery sprouting new life with the start of the wet season.

"I was just joking back there," Tully said, yelling over the engine and the wind. "When I said I wouldn't lose ya out here. I ain't ever lost no one yet. I also haven't brought anyone out here. Which is a technicality, I know. But I didn't wantcha to worry."

"I take it the morbid sense of humour is a Northern Territory thing?" Yelling for conversation wasn't really my favourite way to communicate.

"Can't speak for everyone," he yelled back, that annoyingly cute smirk now a grin. "But it kinda helps to joke about life out here. Go crazy otherwise."

I wanted to ask him if he lived out here but thought I could save that conversation for when we weren't yelling across the car at each other.

An hour out of town, thoroughly windswept and probably sunburned, we turned off the highway onto a road that soon became a track. "Might wanna hold on to the oh-shit bar," he said.

Yes. The permanent smile was now *officially* annoying.

As was the way the wind tousled his hair, and how the way the sunlight made his eyes shine.

Get yourself together. Focus on why you're here.

A serious bump in the track had me reaching for the grab bar across the dash. "Oh shit!"

"Yep. That's how it got its name." Tully laughed. Then he pointed up ahead to another track we were about to pass by. It was a goat track in the scrub. "That's the way we'll go tomorrow."

More of this kind of road? Oh goodie.

"Does this road become impassable in the wet season?" I asked, bouncing around in my seat. I couldn't imagine it getting any worse.

"It's impassable now."

That damn grin.

It was no longer just annoying.

I was beginning to actively dislike it.

"Well, for tourists anyway. When we get down into the lowlands," he went on to say. "When she floods, *then* it's impassable."

"Are we expecting floods?"

"It is the wet season."

Like the skies were listening, it began to spit rain. Fat and heavy droplets at first, then it began to pelt us, but Tully didn't pull over to put the rooftop on. Hell, he didn't even slow down.

Looks like getting drenched was as natural as sitting in the sun to him.

"And how do we navigate through flooded terrain?"

"Just gotta be faster than the rising water." He patted the steering wheel. "She ain't ever let me down yet."

Oh great.

When they'd said he was a wild card, I hadn't realised they meant he was a cowboy with a death wish.

He laughed again and—thankfully—we rounded a bend and, after a small incline, arrived at our first camp-site. He pulled up in an open car shelter, alongside a big Cruiser, behind what looked like an amenities block. From there being another vehicle, I could deduce there were other people here. Or *one* person at least.

He opened his door. "We'll come back for our gear when the rain stops," he said, then made a run for it into the camp. "Come on."

It took a few seconds for me to realise I was expected to follow him. I ran around the corner of the amenities, ducking under the roof and almost running into the back of Tully. He was there with two men, both looked to be in their thirties, both smiling. One of them had short brown hair, sun-kissed skin. The second man had longish black hair and stood back a little.

"This is Jeremiah," Tully said. I was going to correct the full-name thing and suggest they call me Jeremy but figured there was no point. I had a feeling I was going to be Jeremiah for the duration of my stay. Not that I minded. In fact, I probably preferred my full name. "Jeremiah, this is Paul and Derek. They run this place. And they live here."

They lived out here? In the wilderness? Down that road? "You live here?" I asked. "All the way out here?"

Paul laughed and gestured to the wall of water that was rain just a few feet away. "Best address on the planet. But . . ." Then he gestured to the closest cabin. "More specifically, that's our home right there. Tully will look after you tonight, but if there's an emergency, you come find us."

Then Paul clapped Tully on the shoulder. "I put you guys in tent number one. Fridge here is full. You know where everything is. We're gonna be busy for a few hours. If you need us for anything, you don't need us for anything, if you know what I mean."

I wasn't sure what he meant. If we needed him for anything, we didn't need him for anything? That made no sense. But Tully grinned, laughed almost. "Loud and clear."

Paul and Derek disappeared into the pouring rain and into the closest cabin.

Together.

Oh.

Oh wow.

Tully must have seen the look on my face when I connected the dots.

"They run this place," he said again. "Together. They're a couple. Is that a problem?"

I felt my cheeks redden. "No, not at all. Goodness, no. I don't mind. It's great."

Shut up.

For the love of god, shut up.

"Good," he said cheerfully, his smile back in place. "So this is the communal kitchen. We'll probably cook up a BBQ for dinner, I'd reckon. Paul's a pretty good cook."

"But not for a few hours," I mumbled, checking my watch. It was already four o'clock.

Tully laughed, almost louder than the rain on the tin roof.

"But when we're out on our own, we won't have a setup this nice."

I could see now that the camping site was more like a luxury eco-lodge of private tents. The fancy kind with the small wooden decks out front, no doubt nicer than my apartment back in Melbourne.

I hadn't been expecting that.

And when the rain eased up a little, I could see the view.

The rain was moving north, rolling right over us and heading towards the coast, revealing an entire wetland below us. It was a patchwork carpet of green grasses and forest, stitched together with silvery blue rivers.

"Oh wow."

"Glad you like it," Tully said. Then he pointed his chin to the horizon, where the clouds were now dark, where the storms were rumbling. "Because that's where we're going."

Sheets of lightning lit up the clouds, negative charges seeking positive, sheet lightning with crawlers, and cloud-to-ground lightning—an impressive display of nature and destruction.

It made my pulse quicken.

My eyes met Tully's, and I smiled.

CHAPTER THREE
TULLY

DINNER WAS A QUIET AFFAIR, JUST THE FOUR OF US sitting around the communal kitchen. Jeremiah gravitated toward Derek. Once Derek mentioned his telescopes and astronomy, Jeremiah was intrigued.

"Science-minded," Paul said, with an admiring nod toward them both. The sky was dark, the storm long passed, so Derek had his telescope near the edge of the campground, overlooking the wetlands, and he and Jeremiah had been in their own little world for about an hour.

"Does Derek have a limit to the number of questions he allows?" I asked. "Because I think Doctor Jeremiah has far exceeded it."

Paul laughed. "If it's questions about stars and planets, there's never a limit."

I sipped my water and watched them for a while.

"Are you really taking him for a full week?" Paul asked. "That's a long time out there."

I sighed. "Well, I said I normally go for a fortnight, and

he asked if he could tag along. How long he lasts is the real question."

Paul smirked. "Should we take a bet?"

I chuckled. "Probably not."

"Storms are supposed to be bad this summer," he added. "The park has issued warnings, which I assume you know about."

I nodded. "And I explained that to him. He said that's why he's comin' here. Because it's supposed to be bad."

Paul squinted. "Is he sane?"

I snorted. "I'll letcha know in a week."

We watched them for another few moments. "He's kinda cute," Paul mused. "And it'll just be you two, alone?"

I shot him a glance. "Yeah, I know what you're implying, and that's not gonna happen."

He snorted. "Why not? What's a little harmless fun?"

"When is it ever just harmless fun?"

Paul's grin faded into something more serene, his eyes trained on Derek. "When it turns into the love of your life."

I ignored that.

I wasn't the fallin'-in-love kind.

"He's got the bluest eyes I think I've ever seen," Paul added quietly.

That made me look at him. "Right? They're so fuckin' blue. Like a weird dark blue. Could be coloured contacts."

"Doubt it. He doesn't seem the type. Normal contacts, sure. But coloured ones? Nope."

That was true. He didn't seem the type. Not that we knew him at all.

"And he studies lightning," Paul said, almost wistfully. "Like your hobby, but for a job."

He had that implying-tone again. "So?"

"Like a perfect match, dontcha think?"

"No, I don't think."

"Harmless fun, Tully," he said, smiling as he sipped his water.

"About as much harmless fun as getting struck by lightning."

Jeremiah looked back and directly at me, like he'd heard what I'd said. I hoped to god he hadn't heard the whole conversation.

Paul hummed a happy tune, smiling as he drained the last of his water. "Hmm. I think you're in for a whole lotta fun, Tully." He shrugged. "Harmless or not, that's up to you. But can I offer you a suggestion?"

I was certain I didn't want to hear this. "Sure."

"If you're not sure if he's interested and you don't know how to ask, the 'oh no, there's only one bed' thing totally works."

Oh god.

I winced. "We're staying at the bunker. There's only one bed."

Paul laughed. "Of course there is. Just don't pull any of that chivalry shit and take the floor."

I laughed. "Thanks. I'll keep that in mind." I absolutely would not be keeping that in mind. I had no intention of having any fun with Jeremiah, harmless or otherwise. Then something occurred to me . . . "Ah jeez. You didn't take one of the beds outta tent one, did ya?"

Paul grinned. "No. Would you like me to?"

"No thanks. Two is just great."

He sighed and got to his feet. "I'm off to bed. Breakfast's at seven. What time are ya's leaving?"

"We'll probably head out by eight."

"Sounds good."

He said goodnight to the two stargazers, and figuring they'd be studying the stars for a while yet, I left them to it and went into our tent.

It was real nice. One of those fancy glamping tents with white canvas walls and roof, two single beds, a small bathroom, and a little table and chairs. I'd thrown my single duffle bag onto the closest bed, and Jeremiah's bag and big black box were neatly placed at the foot of his bed.

He'd called it his equipment crate. It weighed enough, looked heavy-duty and waterproof, and I had to wonder just what kind of equipment a lightning scientist had. I also had to wonder how he was going to carry it around for his stay. The Jeep would get us most places, but there were some roads too impassable even for me.

It was the beginning of the wet season, after all.

I took a shower, changed into my sleep-boxers. Which were more professional than my sleep-briefs. Or my preference to sleep-naked.

I was pulling back the bedcovers when Jeremiah came in. He stopped when he saw me, averting his eyes away and blushing.

Well damn.

"Oh," he said. "Sorry. I should have knocked."

"It's fine. You should be grateful I put clothes on at all," I joked, but not really. His gaze cut to mine before he hurried to his duffle bag. "I normally wear my birthday suit to bed. Thought I'd dress up a bit for ya."

"Oh well," he said nervously. "I should be grateful. Thank you."

He still wouldn't look at me, so I got into bed and pulled only the sheet up. It was too hot for anything else. "Might wanna take full advantage of the proper shower," I suggested, folding my arms behind my head. "Be the last one for a while."

He gave a nod and took his toiletry bag into the bathroom. I was half asleep when he came back out. He was quiet in the dark as he slipped into his bed, wearing proper sleep shorts and a T-shirt that clung to his chest perfectly. He smelled good, too.

Shaking that thought out of my mind, I settled into sleep.

I absolutely did not dream of harmless fun. Though I did think a jerk off in the shower before breakfast was a good idea. I couldn't risk Jeremiah seeing me with a raging hard-on our first day.

Christ.

This was going to be a long week.

AFTER BREAKFAST, we loaded up the Jeep and went on our way. We had jerry cans of fuel, canisters of water, food supplies, emergency gear, and his equipment crate. The weather would be pretty good up until lunchtime when the humidity and storms would kick in, so we needed to be at our destination by then.

Jeremiah shook hands with Paul and Derek, and with an excited smile, he climbed in. "I'm looking forward to this," he said. He wore more sensible shorts and a looser T-shirt today. I couldn't tell if it was supposed to be expensive vintage or if it was just old, but I got the feeling the outfit he travelled in yesterday was his *good clothes*. I wasn't entirely sure why. His shoes, maybe. They were sensible hiking boots, but not the expensive kind that rich people bought to look the part. His were the kind that poorer people splurged good money on.

I didn't mean that in a bad way.

It's just the Jeremiah who got in my Jeep today seemed like a different Jeremiah to the one who got in yesterday.

The drive was slow going, the road accessible by four-wheel drive only. It was all narrow track, trees and ferns brushing the side of the Jeep, on uneven surfaces, and going very downhill.

"Ugh," he moaned, holding onto the oh-shit bar as we went over a particularly big bump. "You know how I said I was excited to get underway today?"

"Yep."

"I take that back."

"The road'll flatten out some when we get down the ridge," I said.

"Good."

"But then we have water over the roads."

He shot me a bewildered look and I grinned at him. "Excellent," he said, putting his hand flat on the dash to hold himself in his seat. "Do we come back this way? Please say no."

I chuckled. "Nope. We'll be further north by the end of

the trip, and we'll come back from the east, near Arnhem Land. It's flatter out that way."

"You mean we could have gone out that way?" His knuckles were white on the grip bar. "Instead of on this goat track?"

"We could, but where would the fun in that be?" We hit a hole and both of us jolted in our seats. "Plus, this isn't a goat track. It's a wild pig track."

His sharp blue eyes cut to mine. "Your sense of humour is about as funny as this drive."

I grinned at him, but it was lost on him because he didn't look at me. Not until we were on much flatter ground anyway. His fingers uncurled from the grip bar and he finally exhaled. It was still a track, still crowded over by trees and ferns, but flatter.

I slowed the Jeep to a stop.

"Is everything all right?" he asked, alarmed.

"Sure." I pointed back up at the ridge now behind us. "See that gap in the trees on top of the ridgeline? That's Paul and Derek's camp."

"Oh wow."

"It's a hairy climb down," I admitted. "But I saved us a full day's drive."

Jeremiah gave an annoyed sniff but faced the front again. "Some warning would have been nice."

"I did warn you. I said it was impassable."

He turned slowly to face me. "Impassable would imply that the road is not drivable, meaning one is not supposed to drive on it because it's impassable."

"Impassable is not impossible." I grinned at him and,

putting the car in first, began driving again. "Anyway, that's for tourists, not me."

His eyes lasered in on mine, and oooh boy, those dark blue eyes could hold some fire. It didn't help that I found it funny. It certainly didn't help that I found it sexy as hell.

Disgruntled but choosing silence, he pulled out a map, the kind you found in old service stations, and it was probably just as well. Not that we had phone service out there, but it also meant he wasn't looking at me, and it meant that sapphire gaze wasn't trying to burn holes into my head.

The track had evened out, but it didn't mean it was any less bumpy. The huge potholes were now filled with water, their depth—and subsequent amount of bouncing—hard to gauge. I took it slow, not wantin' to break my suspension.

Jeremiah only just seemed to notice. He looked up from his map to the narrow track ahead, then to me. "The fact you're driving with considerably less speed on this horizontal ground compared to the speed you drove down the vertical hillside makes me believe you actually weren't controlling the speed with which we were plummeting down the vertical hill."

I laughed. "Plummeting is a strong word."

"Plunging also works."

"I think expertly navigating is better."

He rolled his eyes. "I think I know where we are," he said, checking the map again. "We have no phone service out here."

"There ain't much of anything out here."

"I have a serious question. What happens if one of us is injured?"

"I have a first aid kit."

"No, seriously."

"I am serious."

"I meant seriously injured. Like a compound fracture. Or if one of us is bitten by . . . well, anything out here."

"Serious answer—the other one drives us out the long flat way. I have a satellite phone for emergencies. We call 000. You'd be surprised, we're about as remote out here as it gets, but there *are* people around. They'll come. And same goes for us. If we get a call from someone for help, we go to them. It's what you do out here."

He nodded, seemingly pleased with this. "Have you ever had an emergency before?"

"Nope. Don't intend to start now. Even though you probably wanna go holdin' metal rods at lightning bolts or somethin' like that."

He smiled. "Something like that."

We hit a particularly big divot in the road and both of us bounced in our seats. He grabbed the oh-shit bar again. "At risk of sounding like a small child, how much further?"

I laughed. "We got a ways to go. We haven't even crossed the river yet."

He stared at me, those blue eyes trying to determine if I was joking or not. "A river? Please tell me it has a bridge."

I snorted. "A bridge out here? You're funny."

He sat back in his seat. "I should start counting regrets and see how many it takes before I tap out."

I burst out laughing. "Regrets? How many are ya up to already?"

"One, coming down that bloody mountain. I'll let you know after the river, if we survive, if it earned a second regret."

I found myself smiling at him. "Well, with a bit of luck, the water won't be too high yet." I knew it wasn't, but I couldn't help playing with him just a little bit. "But if we do get into trouble, whatever you do, don't get out of the Jeep. And if you do end up in the drink, don't cling to any logs." I paused for effect. "Cause those logs are the bitin' kind."

Those blue eyes almost popped right out of his head. "There are crocodiles here?"

I laughed and shook my head. "Just kidding."

He paled and shrank back in his seat. "That was not funny."

I thought it was hilarious. "I mean, it was a little bit," I said as we jostled along.

He held up two fingers. "You. You just became my second regret."

THE RIVERBED WAS FILLING NICELY, but the causeway was still easily passable. It wouldn't be in a week or so. At all. I still took it slow across the causeway; jokes aside, there was no room for stupid mistakes out here.

Jeremiah's hand tightened on the door as he peered out.

"The river will start to come down now. Over the next

two months, we'll get anything up to fifteen hundred millimetres of rain. This whole track'll be underwater for two months. All road access will have to come from the east. Choppers come from Darwin, which is due west from here. And I joked about the crocs before. There won't be any here yet, but when all this is water, this'll be full of them."

"But we don't come back this way," he said, almost to reassure himself.

"No. We don't. And the bunker, the spot where we're staying, is on a rise. Like a plateau. There are no water-ways close by. Unless the rains get real bad."

I stopped short on saying anything else, because the rains were expected to get bad, and he knew this.

It was why he was here.

"But this is Kakadu," he said with a sigh. "The tropical Top End. There are crocodiles."

"True."

"And the place where we're staying," he said. "The bunker. You stay there often?"

"Yep. Once or twice a year."

"How did you find out about it?"

"I used to come out here as a kid. My dad would go hunting . . . well, what they'd call ethical culling. Pigs, buffalo, crocs. When colonies got diseases, or if they got too big or too close to humans. We'd ride in ATVs and heli-copters. It was crazy fun." I smiled at the memories. "We got to know the guides and the rangers over the years, so even when Dad stopped coming, I kept coming back every summer. But not for hunting."

"Why did your dad stop?"

"They don't do the culling anymore. Not like they used to. They move them on now. To different parts of the park and whatnot."

He nodded. "That's probably a good thing."

"Yep. We know more now. About how the ecosystems work."

He was quiet for a while then, watching the scenery, smiling at the birds and the occasional lizard or wallaby.

"Bet it feels a million miles away from Melbourne," I said.

"I was just thinking this feels like Indonesia. Well, except for the wallabies back there."

"We're not far from the coast. About twenty kilometres as the crow flies. You're closer to Indonesia than Melbourne, that's for sure."

He nodded again, only grabbing the grip bar a few more times before the track began to make a noticeable rise, and sure enough, after a few more minutes through the trees and grasses, we entered a clearing and up ahead was our camp.

The *bunker*, as it was known, was no more than a brown tin shed when it was all closed up, and I tried not to smile at the look on Jeremiah's face. "Behold, the Kakadu Hilton," I said, pulling up beside the building and cutting the engine. "Let's get it set up before you declare this to be regret number three."

I climbed out of the Jeep and went straight for the front door. Jeremiah got out slowly, taking in his surroundings. The bunker itself was nothing fancy. It was literally a shed made of steel and concrete, hence the name. But it was built in the '70s, had a concrete floor, a diesel generator for power, a small kitchenette, a pit toilet, and an outdoor shower. There was even a small solar panel for lights.

It was all I ever needed.

"What exactly needs setting up?" Jeremiah asked as I got the door open.

"Let me just check for any unwanted friends first."

Jeremiah froze, his eyes wide.

I flipped the light switch and the overhead light buzzed and clicked a few times before it lit the room up in a yellow-orange glow. A few bugs and insects scurried and scampered, but nothin' slithered.

Not yet, anyway.

I took the long-handled broom and poked and prodded, lifted lids, and then the thin mattress on the bed. I checked the exposed rafters, and I opened the few cupboards. The only thing that greeted me were spiders and dust bunnies. "All clear," I yelled as I walked back out.

Jeremiah hadn't moved an inch.

I withheld the laughter, but I did smile. "Come on, you can help me lift the sides."

"The what?"

"The sides," I said again. "They lift out and up, like wings." I pointed to the side walls where he could now see the bolts. I slid the first bolt out and he did the other end. Then from inside the shed, we pushed the side wall out and up. Metal poles on the ends came down and held the wall up like an awning.

Then we did the other side, and the breeze blew straight through.

"Now that's pretty cool," he said, clearly impressed. He

inspected the giant hinges and the crude welding. It was as sturdy and strong as anything I'd ever seen.

"Made in the '70s, after Cyclone Tracy," I explained. "When they could do shit like this without ten years of red tape and building codes. No way something like this would pass today. But it's classed as an emergency shelter for cyclones, and after Tracy ripped through Darwin, they put a few of these up over the Top End."

"I can see why it's called the bunker." He was frowning up at the long fluorescent light. "Why is the light orange?"

"Well, it's technically yellow," I amended. "Bugs aren't attracted so much to it. If it was a bright white, we'd be swarmed."

When he didn't say anything, I looked over and, sure enough, he was now staring at the bed.

At the very much one and only bed.

"Put your pillow at one end, I'll put mine at the other," I said like it was no big deal. Because it wasn't a big deal. And if he was that opposed to sharing a double bed with a guy, he could damn well sleep on the floor.

"Here, help me lift this," I said, not giving him time to dwell on the bed situation. I took one end of the table, he took the other, and we moved it out under the new roof. "Rain tends to come from the north," I said. "So we can move our stuff to the lee side."

"And this stuff just gets left here?" he asked, looking around. "Unlocked?"

It really wasn't all that great. "Uh, sure. It's a shelter in case of emergencies." I shoved the bed with my boot. "I brought this mattress with me about three years ago. You should have seen the old one." I made a face. "There's a few carcinologists who stay here on the regular, but only after the wet season."

"Carcinologists? What crustaceans live here?"

I was surprised he knew what that was. Then, given he had a doctorate in somethin', I probably shouldn't have been surprised at all. "Not here, exactly. But in the mangroves north of here. They trek in, into the real swamps. The crabs in the mangroves do something special, I dunno what it is though. Something about carbon emissions and the cycle of life and helping with global warming." I shrugged. "They stop here on their way out. And then there's the dry-season folks. It's busier then, but I tend to avoid people so I don't know much about the folks who stay here in the dry season."

I moved the chairs out to the table, giving us some more room. "But the rule is you leave it as you find it. Don't break shit, and keep it clean."

"That works," he said, looking around. "It's actually a lot cleaner than I was expecting. Nothing a good dusting can't fix."

I handed him the broom. "Don't let me stop ya."

He made himself busy sweeping and brushing spiderwebs down, dusting, and then he decided to wash everything in the small kitchen with soapy water before we unpacked the Jeep. He didn't seem opposed to hard work, and I liked that about him. He just got stuck in and got shit done.

While he was doing all that, I checked the bathroom and the pit toilet, made sure the water tanks were all in good order and free of creepy crawlies and unwanted critters. I boiled some water on the gas stovetop for cooking and brushing our teeth. By mid-afternoon, we had our camp set up.

Exhausted, I flopped down on the bed, but Jeremiah pulled his equipment crate over and started pulling everything out, takin' inventory and checking it all over. He picked up one piece, a box of some type, then another. He laid it all out on the table, neat and methodical.

"Hey, Jeremiah," I said. "How'd you get into all this? I mean, why lightning?"

He stopped, sitting still for a long few seconds. "I've always been fascinated by it," he said quietly; a frown marred his brow, a flinch almost, and his demeanour changed. "For as long as I can remember."

What an odd reaction.

There was no way that was the whole truth. There was definitely more to the Jeremiah Overton story than he was letting on.

Hmm.

Interesting.

CHAPTER FOUR

JEREMIAH

I LIKED TULLY. PROBABLY MORE THAN I LIKED MOST people. He was a 'what you see is what you get' kind of guy, and I appreciated that. He had a wild sense of humour that I still didn't entirely understand, but he was bright and always smiling. Completely carefree.

If sunshine was a person, it would be Tully Larson.

Well, if sunshine with a side of unpredictable was a person.

But I didn't know him well enough, or at all, really, to be telling him the ins and outs of my life.

When he'd asked why I studied lightning, I told him the truth. It had fascinated me. My entire life. That wasn't a lie.

Thankfully he hadn't asked *why* it fascinated me.

He just took my answer as gospel and moved on. Maybe he didn't care either way. Maybe he was just making polite conversation. We were stuck out here alone together, in the middle of freaking nowhere, for a long time, after all.

"What's that thing for?" Tully asked, getting up off the bed and taking a seat at the table.

Oh dear.

I sighed. "And we were doing so well."

His eyes cut to mine. "What do you mean?"

"With the lack of questions. We were doing so well."

He laughed and picked up the deploy system and looked it over. "What does this thing do? It looks like a gas cylinder?"

I took it off him and put it back on the table. "It's a quick deploy system. It screws into the automated weather station, measures wind speeds, pressure, temperatures."

"Cool." He went to grab the small solar panel and I took it before he could. "Please don't touch. This equipment is expensive, and it's all I've got."

"I'm not gonna break it," he said, pouting like a child.

People rarely ever *mean* to break things. But things get dropped by accident, and good intentions can't fix broken equipment, and I certainly couldn't afford to replace anything.

I took out the laptop and opened it. "What are the chances of a decent signal here?"

Tully snorted and held up two fingers. "Buckley's and none."

I thought as much. "That's okay. I can still record data. And just hope nothing happens to the unit before I can send it to the cloud, that's all."

Tully shrugged. "We can drive out every morning if you need. Just a couple of miles to see if we can get a better signal. You can upload your data every day that way."

I smiled at him, regretting how I'd scolded him when he was just trying to be helpful. "That'd be great, thanks."

I fired the laptop up, entered in the location information, and in a few moments, the screen was full of a weather radar and changing stats.

"Oh, that's cool," Tully said. I shot him a look and he put his hands up. "I'm not gonna touch it. Show me what it does."

"It's from the geostationary op satellite," I explained. "There are satellites each equipped with GLM, which is Geostationary Lightning Maps, that detects the light emissions from both cloud-to-ground and inter-cloud lightning which escape the cloud and make it to space. This technology helps severe weather forecasters identify rapidly intensifying thunderstorms so they can issue accurate and timely severe thunderstorm, and cyclone warnings, for example."

He snorted. "And what's the dumb version?"

"The satellites read data and track electrical storms."

"Right. Why didn't you just say that?"

"I did."

"I can assure you, you did not."

I sighed. "The bureau radars," I said, changing topics and changing tabs on the computer, bringing up a different radar, "are different. It's just reading data fed from local weather stations in Darwin and Warruwi." I looked at the numbers. "Well, it's trying to. It's searching, lagging, mostly."

"But the radar? Is that current?"

"No. It's lagging too." I went through the equipment crate and pulled out a booster. It looked like an antenna. I hooked it up to the converter, then plugged it into the laptop. "I need to find somewhere . . ."

He groaned. "Gaaah, why didn't you say you had a booster? I can put it on the roof for ya," Tully said, grinning. "Would that help?"

"Well, it would, actually. Very much."

His face lit up, as if being helpful was his favourite thing to do. He went out and looked up at the roof, and I followed. God, the sun had some bite, and the humidity was stifling. The bunker was surprisingly cool. "What about up there," he said, pointing to the highest pitch of the roof. "Lemme grab the ladder."

He found a ladder around the side of the bunker and I held it as he climbed, not at all looking at his muscular legs as he went up. "I'm very glad to see there are lightning rods installed," I said, seeing the metal diversion rods installed along the ridgeline.

"Yeah, they didn't muck around when they built this thing," he said, getting to the top. "Holy shit this roof's hot," he mumbled, but I held up the booster and he grinned as he took it from me. "Go and look on the screen and tell me when the signal's better."

"The cord isn't very long. I'll have to move the table. Sorry!" I tried to hurry because I didn't want him to burn himself on the hot tin roof, but it did give him more cord. He moved the booster and I checked the screen.

"How about now?" he called out.

It was better but still not great. "No."

The cord pulled up some more and I could hear him move further along the roof. "How about n—"

"Stop there! That's good!" I went back out so I could see him. "It's good now, thank you."

"We'll run the cord down the corner so we can close up the walls if we need, and I'll have to rig up a bracket or a brace," he said. "As soon as the wind and storms start, it's not gonna stay put."

He began to climb back down the ladder, and I was very much aware of how remote and isolated we were out here. "Please be careful," I said, again deliberately not looking at his legs as he came down.

He got to ground level and was grinning at me, like he could tell I was making an effort to divert my eyes. "You all good there?"

"Yes, I just didn't want you to fall," I said, ignoring the innuendo in his tone. "You may be fine in a medical emergency if I'm the injured one, but if it's you that's injured and you're depending on me to be cool, calm, and collected, you're bound to be disappointed. And in a lot of pain."

He laughed and clapped my shoulder. "You'd be fine." But then he went about scavenging up some wood and the lid of an old plastic container in a row of discarded materials on the ground at the end of the bunker. He found what he was after, somehow made it work, zip-tied it all together to make a little raft-looking device, shoved some more zip ties in his mouth and went back up the ladder.

I stood out in the sun to try and see what he was doing but the direct heat got too much for me. There were a few bangs, some mumbles, and some colourful cursing, then a victorious grin. "Pass me up my phone."

I found it on the bed and passed it up to him. This

time, when he climbed down, his grin was even wider. "Just call me MacGyver," he said, showing me the photos he'd just taken.

There, zip-tied to the metal ridging on the roof, was a little wooden raft with my booster zip-tied to it. It made me laugh. "Good job, MacGyver." Then I noticed how sweaty he was. "Come in and have a drink of cold water."

"Yeah, it's gettin' hot out there. It's gettin' dark over the north-west too. I'd reckon the storm this arvo's gonna be a doozy."

I checked the radar on the laptop—seeing it was now in real-time—and turned it so he could see the band of yellow and red moving across the map. "I think you're right."

He clapped his hands together. "Hell yes."

It was rare to meet someone who shared my enthusiasm, and I found myself smiling at him. "I need to get my gear organised."

"I could help," he said, hopeful. "If I was allowed to touch anything."

I rolled my eyes but relented. "Fine."

That wild grin was back. "Awesome. I'll be the best fulminologist assistant to ever fulminology assist."

I sighed, pretending to be annoyed.

It was actually kind of sweet and fun to be doing this with someone else. I'd been working alone for so long, I wasn't used to having company in the field.

Tully picked up the small metal box. "Okay, so what does this thing do?"

I sighed again, for real this time, and tried to be patient with his inquisitiveness. It could have been worse. He could have been a real jerk, or a horrible person. But he wasn't. He was kind and curious.

And cute.

"It's the housing unit for the data logger, power supply and modem for the auto-station. Waterproof, of course."

He pointed to something else, having learned not to touch it. "And this?"

"It's the solar radiation sensor."

"What's this camera for?"

"It's a secondary unit," I explained. "The automatic weather station has a limited scope, so I like to focus a second camera on the unit itself so we can see the effect the storm is having from both perspectives."

He looked at it in complete wonder, excited. "That is all so freakin' cool."

I found myself smiling at him again. "Yeah. It is."

———

THE STORM HIT AT four fifteen, and even though it hit hard, it was a relief. Humidity sat over 90% for almost an hour before it broke, sweat was running down my back and dripping down my face. It was almost unbearable.

When Tully pulled his shirt off, I was going to complain but then thought better of it. It wasn't hurting anyone, and it was for his comfort, after all.

At least that's what I told myself.

It had nothing to do with his ripped physique, broad shoulders, defined pecs and abs, tanned skin, or the hair on his chest.

It had nothing to do with that at all.

Keep telling yourself that.

We lowered the walls a little, not all the way, but just so the rain wouldn't come in. The design of this shed was so simple yet genius, it was hard not to be impressed. It withstood the storm as if it were no more than a gentle breeze, let alone the thirty millimetres of water it dumped in the sixty-kilometre winds.

Thunder boomed and cracked, lightning lit up the sky in jagged cracks and bolts. It was a decent display and I managed some recordings, but it wasn't anything extraordinary.

The electrical readings weren't as high as I'd liked—it was mostly sheet lightning, intra-cloud, with little cloud-to-ground activity—but it was a good test for a first run.

A good taste of what was to come, perhaps.

And it was good to see how Tully reacted. He was so interested in the radar and the readings, and what both cameras recorded. The thunder clapped overhead a few times, loud enough to ring in my ears. The clouds were low, and the electrical charge readings were constant, which meant we were right in the thick of it.

"Is that high?" he yelled over the sound of the rain.

I see-sawed my hand. "No. It means we're close, but it's not bad or threatening at all," I explained. "It's pretty tame."

He nodded, but his grin was still there. I was pretty sure he just liked storms. He didn't care about the science behind it, he just liked the wildness of it.

When the storm had passed and the rain cleared, we opened up the walls again, letting the breeze through. It was much cooler now.

"Listen to that noise," Tully said, staring into the trees.

I didn't need to perk my ears at all. The sounds of the forest were almost deafening. Cicadas, frogs, birds sang a cacophony of song.

"It's a good sign, right?" I asked.

"Yep. Did you know birds sing a different sound after rain than what it is before the rain?"

"No, I didn't know that."

"It's pretty cool." He shrugged. "If you know what to listen for. One of the old guys that used to go huntin' with my dad told us that. He could tell the difference in bird-song. I can't. But he also said if you don't hear any birds before a bad storm,"—he gestured to the trees—"you know it's time to bail out."

"Yes, I've heard that," I admitted. "I did a study in South America a few years ago now. The field guides said the same thing. Listen to the forest."

He was clearly surprised. "South America, huh? Where else have you been storm chasing?"

Storm chasing . . .

"I don't chase storms," I said. I knew he meant no harm, but still . . . the demeaning generalisation stung. "I study fulminology."

Tully shrugged. "So where else have you studied the science of fulminology?"

Now I felt petulant.

"Just two places. Indonesia and South America. Venezuela to be exact. There's a place called Catatumbo—"

"Ah, the House of Thunder," Tully said, his smile back in place. "I've heard it's amazing."

I don't know why it surprised me that he knew of it. He was a storm chaser, after all.

"Yes, the lightning display is amazing. It's an atmospheric phenomenon that really has to be seen to be believed."

"When did you go there?"

"For my final thesis, I did a study there."

Tully sighed. "Must be amazing getting to travel the world to see all the different storms."

"I certainly couldn't afford to go on my own." I didn't know why I was telling him this. "Same with this expedition; I obtained a grant through the bureau. I was very lucky . . ."

"Still exciting though."

I gave a nod. "Yes, it is."

"And your work at the bureau? What do you do there?"

"High impact weather, aviation hazards, radar science and nowcasting, forecast systems, statistical post-processing, forecast verification. Those kinds of things. There is also a cross-data interaction with climate change and variability, with projections and predictions."

"Sounds . . . boring."

I almost smiled. "To some."

"Ah, come on, you gotta admit field trips are always more fun than theory, right?"

"I never hated the theory lessons."

"Of course you didn't." When I glanced his way, he was smiling at me. I resisted sighing, barely. His annoying grin widened. "Soooo," he said, "what are you actually hoping to find in this study? Is it just lightning in general? Or is there a specific theory you want to test?"

"I have . . ." I tried again. "The causation of strikes and the predictability; a study which would increase the ability to predict where lightning will strike, and perhaps the ability to direct the strike to a more favourable location, amongst other things. Not just for preventative measures, but also a better understanding of lightning activity from all around the world enables policy makers, government agencies, and meteorology departments to make more informed decisions related to weather and climate." That well-rehearsed line sounded flat, even to my ears. "Though mostly they choose to ignore anything climate related."

His brow creased and confusion crossed in his eyes. "Don't they do that already? Not the ignoring climate data. We know that. But the predictions, with the metal rods on buildings, like this one." He pointed to the ceiling. "They don't offer protection, as such, but channel the strike to a point and divert the current to the ground."

I should have known I couldn't fool him.

"Well, yes. That's correct. But I'm not talking about diverting strikes away from one building. I'm talking about densely populated areas in general."

"Well, that's cool. But what do you really want to study lightning for?" He grinned, charming and cute. "Not the spiel you just gave me that probably smoothed over your faculty grant application admin. What are you *really* studying? What drives you to travel the world chasing lightning?"

My gaze shot to his, and the truth just rolled right off my tongue.

"I want to study the effects a lightning strike has on the human body. The causation, the predictability, the reason . . ." I stopped short and made myself breathe, regroup. "By studying lightning, I can better understand the basic principles of who, what, why, and where of future strikes."

He stared at me, somewhat bewildered. Then he scoffed and shook his head. "Please tell me you're not gonna wrap yourself up in foil and go stand out in the middle of the clearing hopin' to get struck," he said with a laugh.

"No, of course not," I mumbled. "I'm not going to wrap myself in foil."

He chuckled but then his smile slowly died. "But you're not going to try and get yourself electrocuted, are you? Foil or no foil."

I shook my head and concentrated on the laptop. "That's absurd." I ignored how he was staring at me. "I need to fill in my report."

"Jeremiah?" His tone was curt with warning. "I didn't bring you out here on a suicide mission."

I looked up from the screen and turned to face him. "Good. Because I don't intend to die."

"But you do intend to use yourself as an experiment."

And that was a possibility I couldn't deny.

CHAPTER FIVE

TULLY

Jeremiah Overton was in-fucking-sane.

He went about fillin' in his reports and doing statistics and numbers while I tried to get my head around what he'd just said.

He wanted to study the effects of lightning strikes on a human body, and when I'd questioned if he intended to use himself as a test bunny, he hadn't denied it.

The more I thought about it, the more it bothered me. "Isn't that morbid curiosity?" I asked. "Wanting to know what it does to the human body?"

"It's a medical science. Keraunomedicine is the medical study of lightning casualties." He shrugged.

"So why didn't you become the other kind of doctor and do that kera-nom-whatever you called it medicine?"

"Because I'd have to understand lightning first. Which is why I do this." He made a face, then gave me another well-practiced spiel. "To best predict lightning strikes and possibly save lives, first we have to understand it, right?"

Hmm. "True."

I guess.

"Why do you love storms so much?" he asked, turning the conversation on me as if it was proving that I, too, was morbidly curious.

"I told ya before. I love the ferocity of them, being completely at the mercy of nature. It's terrifying and magnificent. And it's one helluva adrenaline rush."

He raised one eyebrow as if that did prove his point, and I dunno . . . maybe it did.

"Couldn't you just go skydiving for that thrill?" he countered.

"I could." I thought about it for a while. "And being out here reminds me of my childhood, hangin' out with my dad, doing wild-boy shit. That's what my mum used to call it."

He frowned then and paused with his mouth open, as if he was trying to find the right words. But in the end, he decided on saying nothing at all.

Maybe he wasn't sure how to ask such personal questions.

"My mum still calls it wild-boy shit," I added, hoping it would make it easier for him. "Every year when I come out here, she shakes her head at me."

He packed up some of his gear, clearing away half the table, and he stayed silent so long I wondered if he'd heard me at all. But then he asked, "Do you have any brothers and sisters?"

"I'm the youngest of four. Two brothers, Rowan and Ellis. They're ten and four years older than me. And my sister, Zoe. She's seven years older than me. I'm closest with Ellis. The oldest two got lumped with the parental expectations to take over the family business," I said with a laugh. "Just kidding. We all work for the family company. But I'm the youngest, the most spoilt, and clearly the favourite. Also the best looking, and the funniest."

He smirked, thankfully understanding that I was joking. "And the most modest, I see."

I grinned at him. "Modesty is not a family trait, sorry. What about your family? Are you all geniuses? Or did you get all the brains *and* looks in your family too?"

His smile faltered and he turned back to his gear, a small black box in his hand seemingly forgotten. "It's just been me and my dad since I can remember. He . . . he, uh . . ." he put the box back in the crate. "He doesn't understand why I do what I do. He says if I'm so smart, I should have become a 'real' doctor." He used air quotes and then rolled his eyes. "God, could you imagine? One, I hate blood. And two, I don't like people. Why on earth would I want to help them?"

That made me laugh. I was glad his sullen mood didn't last long.

"So you *do* work?" he asked. "You're not just some lucky guy who doesn't have to work who gets to be a full-time storm chaser?"

I snorted out a laugh. "I wish. Yeah, I work. I do have flexibility. Like I said, it's the family business, so I can take time when I want. As long as I've earned it. I'm not an actual freeloader. I tried to be, but they wouldn't let me."

That earned me half a smile. "What is the family business?"

"Shipping. Imports, exports."

"Oh. Nice."

Something about his tone told me he didn't think that was nice at all, and I wasn't sure what to say about that. I decided a change of topic was in order.

"So, if your interest is in people getting struck by lightning, why don't you go to where the most occur? Like Africa."

"You seem to have the preconceived idea and highly deluded notion that there is money in academia that would allow such travels."

I snorted.

"We know *why* lightning happens," he added. "Abundant moisture and the mountainous terrain help initiate thunderstorms. That's why places like Africa, Central America, Asia, and Brunei experience the highest densities of strikes per square kilometre. Global patterns follow the equatorial band, more or less. Tropical storms, with high temperatures, high humidity; it makes sense. But lightning is still largely an unknown entity. We think we understand it, and we can grapple with the physics of lightning, but it's unpredictable and dangerous, and—"

"And that's why you love it."

His gaze cut to mine. "I don't love it. Far from it. I just want to understand it." His voice was quiet, so final, there was nothing I could add. He made himself busy looking at data readouts, so I lit up the citronella candles and plugged in the vibration poles at the four corners of the shed.

"What are they?" Jeremiah asked, watching me.

"Critter deterrents," I replied. "Snakes, mostly. The poles go into the ground like a tent peg and emit a low frequency vibration pulse. It keeps snakes away, but also goannas and other uninvited friendlies. Spiders don't like it much either."

"Good," he said, looking suspiciously up at the ceiling rafters, then his eyes drifted back to the bed. "And the netting thing?"

"We roll it down of a night. The mozzies are big enough to carry you outta here."

He made a face. "Oh great."

I put a can of bug repellent spray on the table. "This is your friend. It stinks but it works." I left him to it and made a start on dinner. "I hope you like beef and rice," I said. "Because we'll be eating it a lot."

"Oh yeah, that sounds great, actually."

I'd mastered the one-pot rice and beef in my time camping. I'd throw in some veggies or beans, and when I was sick of it, I'd add in different flavours and spices. I'd never much cared for cuisine. I'd just needed to feed myself enough of something to sustain me; I never needed anything fancy. Jeremiah didn't seem to be the fancy type, but after a week of eating the same thing, he might not be so thankful.

When I handed him a bowl, he took it with a smile. "Oh, wow. Thank you." He shovelled in the first few mouthfuls like he was starving. "This is really good!"

I chuckled. "We'll see if you're saying that at the end of the week."

He demolished his dinner, and it surprised me just how much he could put away. "I'll wash up," he said, taking my empty bowl. "Fair's fair."

I watched him at the makeshift sink for a while, with the pump faucet and having to boil water on the gas stove, letting him figure how to use it. He managed just fine. "How was the data you collected?" I asked.

"It was okay." He wiped his brow with his shirtsleeve. "Jeez, it's hot. The humidity is brutal."

I smirked at him. "Yeah. You get used to it."

"Have you lived in Darwin your whole life?"

"Yep. Where the only two seasons we have are hot and really fucking hot."

He finished washing up, then lifted the hem of his shirt up to wipe his face, giving me a great view of his waist. Trim, muscular even, which I did *not* expect, and a trail of dark hair from his navel down to his . . .

He cleared his throat.

I shrugged, not one bit sorry. "If you're hot, take your shirt off. Hell, get around in your undies. I don't care."

He made a face. "I might take a shower," he mumbled, quickly taking his toiletries and towel with him.

"Okay," I replied, even though he didn't appear to hear me.

I heard him mumble to himself, then I heard the water . . .

And then a scream that had me up and off the chair, racing for the door. Jeremiah burst out of the bathroom stall, grappling with a towel barely wrapped around his waist. He was pale and panting, now standing beside the bed, as far as he could get from the bathroom.

"What is it?" I asked, reaching for the broom.

He shook his head.

I poked my head in, gingerly peeking into the shower cubicle, expecting to see a snake . . . only to find a rather large green tree frog up near the water tank.

I went back out. Jeremiah had fixed the towel around his waist, which was disappointing, to say the least. He was still pale, his eyes wide. "The frog?"

His nostrils flared, his jaw clenched. "They have. Suction cups. For feet!"

I would have laughed if he didn't look like he was about to puke.

"Please get rid of it," he said quickly. "I don't care how or what you do with it. Just please get rid of it."

"Okay," I said, leaning the broom against the wall. I picked up the frog, and walking out into the clearing, I let him go. "Go find somewhere else to call home, little buddy."

When I went back into the shed, Jeremiah hadn't moved. He shuffled from one foot to the other. "Can you please check the shower? Actually, you know what? Never mind. I'll wait until tomorrow. In the daylight. Or maybe I just won't shower at all for the entire duration of our stay. I can stand in the rain tomorrow. It's fine."

I had to chew on my bottom lip to stop from smiling. "I checked the water tank earlier," I said. "There were no frogs in it. He must have just joined you."

He shuddered.

"Let me get your things," I said, collecting his toiletries and clothes, and walked over to him.

He swallowed hard as he took them. "Thank you." Then he lifted his chin, proud and defiant. "I'm sure you have a joke or something you'd like to say. Maybe sing the 'Jeremiah was a Bullfrog' line. It wouldn't be the first time I've heard it."

I gave his shoulder a squeeze, ignoring the fact that he

was very naked under that towel. "There ain't nothing funny about phobias," I said.

His eyes searched mine, and maybe he was looking for the punchline. He wouldn't find one.

"Thank you," he whispered, clutching his clothes.

"Gotta say, though," I said brightly, waving him up and down. "You're more ripped than I assumed a scientist would be."

He scowled at me then pulled his shirt back on. "Do you make inappropriate comments to all your visitors?"

"Only the really hot ones."

He stared at me.

It made me laugh. "Just kidding. I told ya before, I ain't ever brought anyone out here."

He grumbled under his breath, then pulled his shorts on under his towel, then finally pulled it free. He was still scowling at me but he sighed. "Well . . . thank you for getting rid of the . . ." He waved his hand in the direction of the bathroom.

"No problem. I'll try and rig up something for ya tomorrow," I said. "To stop any uninviteds from tryin' to catch a lucky peek at ya."

He clearly chose not to reply to that. "Well, if you don't mind, I'll have to brush my teeth out here."

"That's fine. Take a cup of the water I boiled earlier and spit it outside."

"Oh." He made a visible effort to compose himself. "Good idea."

I decided to take a quick shower, absent any frogs, and I came out wearing just my boxer shorts. If my shirtlessness bothered him, he'd have to get used to it. It was freaking hot.

He was unrolling the fly net above the bed and he stalled when he saw me. He checked me out, like he did the night before when I wore just boxers to bed and like he did when I took my shirt off in the afternoon.

He could deny it all he liked, but I knew what I saw.

His eyes on me when he thought I weren't looking. Raking over my chest, my back. I weren't blind, and I weren't stupid.

I knew appreciation when I saw it.

"Here," I said, standing on the other side of the bed. I reached for the rolled-up netting. "Let me get this side."

He was quiet and didn't speak much as we got ready for bed. He made sure his pillow was as far over as it could be, our sleeping spaces as separate as the bed allowed. He sat on the furthest edge he possibly could.

"I can sleep in the Jeep if you'd prefer," I offered. I switched on my LED lantern and turned off the overhead light.

"No, it's fine. You'd have no mosquito protection and . . ." He swallowed hard. "I think I'd prefer you in here. If I wake up to a freaking monitor lizard going through our camp, I'll need you close by."

I chuckled as I lay down. "Nice to know I'm good for somethin'."

He slowly lay down, stiff and trying not to take up too much space.

"Ever shared a bed with a man before?" I asked.

He turned his head so fast to look at me, his blue eyes stark in the darkness. "What's that supposed to mean?"

I snorted and put my arms behind my head. "Just askin'. You look petrified, like you think I'm about to jump ya bones or something."

"I am not." He turned back to stare at the ceiling, huffing indignantly. "And for your information, I have shared a bed with . . . none of your business."

I chuckled. I knew it. I knew from the way he'd been looking at me that he was inclined, or curious at the very least.

"Good to know. And for the record, so we're even," I said. "I've shared a bed with a man before too."

I noticed his hands curl into fists by his side. "Well, that's . . . good for you and none of my business."

He was so easy to rattle. I shuffled onto my side so I could look at him, one arm tucked up under my head. "Okay, so super important question time," I said.

He was silent and stock-still, waiting . . .

"What's your favourite dinosaur?"

He stared at the ceiling, then blinked, then looked at me. "What?"

"Your favourite dinosaur," I repeated. "Everyone has one, they just don't talk about it."

"Umm," he hesitated, shaking his head. "I don't know. I haven't thought about it."

"Not even when you were a kid? Everyone has a favourite dinosaur when they're a kid. Mine's the Supersaurus. The biggest dinosaur to ever live. Most people say the T-Rex or a raptor or something, because they're cool. But the Supersaurus is so overlooked. They're huge. Like fuckin' massive. And gentle, and herbivores. And you know, T-Rex's and raptors are cool in a screeching violent-rampage kinda way, I guess. But the good ol' gentle giants are where it's at. Imagine being as big as a football field and not choosing violence."

When I turned to look at him, he was smiling. But he didn't say anything. Maybe he thought it was stupid or childish . . . whatever.

I sighed and closed my eyes.

Jeremiah was quiet and I was drifting off to sleep when he spoke. "The Quetzalcoatlus. It was a pterosaur, a flying dinosaur. As tall as a giraffe with wings like a bat and a long needle-like beak as long as a car."

I stared at him. "Jesus Christ. That's not fucking terrifying at all."

He laughed, more relaxed now, and I smiled as I drifted off to sleep.

CHAPTER SIX

JEREMIAH

TULLY SPENT THE ENTIRE MORNING RIGGING UP some kind of netting over the shower stall and the water tank that fed the shower. His concern over my phobia of frogs was a nice change to the usual ridicule I received, and it was poor judgement on my behalf to assume he would have laughed at me.

Tully wasn't like the others.

He wasn't like anyone I'd ever met.

He learned of my phobia and fixed the problem. When he knew my aerial booster would need to go on the roof, he made a bracket for it and MacGyvered it to the roof. He just scooted himself up on to the roof, banged and clanged, swore a bit, sang off key at one point, but he fixed my problems.

No requests, no point to be made, no accolades.

He was incredibly easy to be around.

And him asking me about my favourite dinosaur? It was so unexpected and purely an exercise in helping me relax. I hadn't expected to be sharing a bed with my guide on this trip, and him asking me if I'd shared a bed with a man before was purely him scoping for information. I'd clearly not been as stealthy in appreciating his shirtless torso as I'd thought I'd been.

He'd noticed me staring, obviously. And he wanted to know what that meant, because . . .

Well, I wasn't sure why.

Because he'd shared a bed with men before. And he wasn't talking about camping, that much was clear. No, he'd asked because he'd wanted to know if I was gay or bi or . . . if I'd be so inclined?

Or if I'd be interested?

Hm.

He was definitely not my usual type. I'd always found myself in the company of fellow academics, those who I'd met and talked science with, and sometimes took to my bed, or me to theirs. It was never anything more than a calculated exchange.

But Tully was different. Wild, carefree, kind, and funny. Gorgeous.

And sleeping next to him had been disconcerting.

He'd fallen asleep long before I had, and I'd found myself watching him. The way the night illuminated his features—the waves of his hair, the rise of his cheekbone, the purse of his lips.

He'd even smiled when he dreamed.

So yes, this was presenting a rather peculiar problem. Because if he wanted to know if I was interested, I wasn't certain if I could lie and say no.

My mind was running all kinds of diagnostics on that scenario.

"Somethin' wrong with the laptop?"

His voice startled me. "Oh, uh . . ."

I put the pen down on the table—I wasn't even aware I was holding it—and tapped the space bar on the keyboard. I'd zoned out for so long it had shut down. "No, it's fine. Have you finished already?"

"Yep," he said, sipping his water. He was already sweating.

Already shirtless.

The way his chest glistened . . .

When his smirk became a grin, I knew I'd been caught staring again.

Dammit.

He smiled as he lifted his bottle to his lips. "The netting is over the water tank that feeds the shower. That water comes off the roof and the gutter guards should help, but frogs are pesky little buggers. I also added some dish soap to the tank to keep the mozzies out. The larvae can make you sick, so just be sure to only drink boiled water."

I nodded. "Yes, thank you. And thank you for putting the netting up. I really do appreciate that."

"No problem." He nodded toward the bathroom. "You can have a shower now. Amphibian-free, I promise."

I grimaced at the memory from last night. The big green slimy thing had been ready to jump . . .

But a shower did sound good.

I took my toiletries and towel and after a thorough inspection of the shower cubicle—before stripping this time—I showered.

There was no hot water. It wasn't required. The water was lukewarm at room temperature, but it felt good to scrub the sweat and dirt off, and I felt more awake afterwards. I pulled on the same shorts with a fresh T-shirt and hung my towel over the back of a chair.

I was ready to focus now and not get side-tracked by a certain shirtless man who was now lazing on the middle of the bed, reading something on his phone. "The network gods are shining on us. We have one bar." He turned his phone around to show me the radar on his screen. "From your esteemed colleagues at the Bureau of Meteorology, this afternoon's storm shall hit around half three. Not much activity where we are, though, unless you wanna head up north a bit. Just for the storm."

I checked the laptop and, sure enough, the precipitable satellite information relayed similar information. "How's the road north of here?" I asked.

He rolled onto his side, propped himself up on one elbow, and shot that grin at me that told me the road was hellish.

So I rephrased my question. "Is it worse than the pig track we came down the mountain on?"

"Nah. It's flat, mostly. About ten k's from here we meet the South Alligator River."

"Alligators?"

"There ain't no alligators here. The folks who made the white man maps way back when couldn't tell the difference between gators and crocs."

"But there's crocs," I mumbled. Because of course there would be.

"We'll follow the river along and she winds north, and that's about as far as we can go. Without a boat."

I made a face. I wasn't a fan of boats.

But I did trust Tully. Sure, he was a bit wild, but he'd been coming out here for years. He wouldn't do anything needlessly reckless.

"Okay, let's do it."

He jumped up off the bed and clapped his hands together, that ridiculous smile now a grin.

I was beginning to like his smile again, and if my brain had a weather warning siren like my equipment did, it'd be blaring at full volume, red lights flashing.

Because his smile was contagious, and the spark in his eyes did absurd things to my belly. And the logical part of my brain knew I was heading for trouble, but my heart didn't seem to care.

WHEN TULLY SAID the road north was mostly flat, he was partly right. Gradationally speaking, yes. But flat as in smooth, no.

The road was another track, and while we didn't climb anymore hills or ridgelines, it was filled with holes, divots, and gullies—all filled with varying depths of mud and water. He handled them expertly while I bounced around, tethered to the Jeep only by my white-knuckled grip on the oh-shit bar.

We bounced, slid, and sped our way north to the river just as he'd said. It was surprisingly pretty and moving faster than I thought it would be.

"She's not normally this full," he said. "In the dry season, we could drive across here. And by the end of the wet season, where we are right now, we'd be two metres under water."

Jesus.

Then he pointed to the river ahead of us. "See that?"

See what?

I searched the water, not knowing what to even look for. Having a fair idea what he was going to say and dreading it just the same . . . and then I saw a crocodile slither from the bank into the water, just thirty metres in front of us.

"Oh my god."

He grinned. "Those are the logs that bite. You don't wanna go touchin' those."

I rolled my eyes and tried to exhale. My hands were now numb from holding on so tight. I wanted to ask what we'd do if we broke down here, but I didn't trust my voice to speak.

And I was pretty sure I didn't want to know.

"You'll be fine," he said, his grin not such a comfort now.

He followed the river along, heading north, which meant given I was on the left side of the Jeep, I was closest to the river the whole way. I saw a few more crocodiles, mostly just ripples in the river and suspicious looking logs that sank slowly below the surface as we drove past. But there was also an array of bird life that swarmed the trees and flew overhead. So as terrifying as the crocodiles were, the wet season also brought with it renewed life.

It was all very beautiful.

Soon enough the river began to deviate northwest, heading to the ocean no doubt, and the track we were on swung northeast. The further we went, the further we were away from the crocodiles, but also the better the road condition.

"How's this road for ya?" Tully asked over the sound of the engine.

"Much better," I replied. "It doesn't make me want to vomit."

He laughed, because of course he did.

Then he slowed right down and took a turn that led through thick brush growth with swampy brackish water either side of the track which, thankfully, came to its natural end in a large clearing. He cut the engine and jumped out. "Okay, this is us."

"Here?"

He looked around. "Sure. I'd reckon from your super-duper map, this'll put us right in the path of your storm."

The area itself was almost as big as a football field, and it certainly couldn't have been cleared naturally. "What is this place?"

"Pretty sure it was a mining test site," he said, pulling gear out of the Jeep.

It rankled with me that they'd allow such things in national parks, but perhaps that was a conversation for a different time.

"Yeah, I know," Tully added, putting my equipment crate on the ground. "Don't get me started on it. Mining corp money speaks a different language, apparently."

I mustn't have been able to hide my annoyance as much as I thought, but I was glad we held similar opinions. "Hm, yes, well." I huffed, wiping the sweat from my brow. "Jeesh, it's sweltering today."

"The humidity's a killer." Tully threw a bottle of water to me. "Keep hydrated."

He had a shirt on now, probably to save his skin from the direct sun, and it clung to him in the best of ways . . . until I realised mine was clinging to me as well. I fanned the hem, trying to get some air moving.

"You can take it off," Tully said, nodding to my chest. "Your shirt. I won't mind."

I sniffed and wiped my face with the bottom half of my shirt instead. "No thanks. I'm not a prude. I'm just prone to sunburn and I'd rather not make myself ill."

His smirk was sly and filthy. "I can apply sunscreen all over. It's my duty as your guide, you know. To make sure you don't burn."

"I'm fine, thank you," I said, ignoring the thrill his offer gave me.

Was he flirting?

God, I think he's flirting.

He walked over to me, studying my face. "Are you burned already? Looking a bit red in the cheeks, there."

That wasn't flirting. That was patronising.

I glowered at him. "I'm hot and bothered, that's all."

He grinned. "I can help with that too."

Jesus.

I picked up the portable weather station tripod and shoved it in his hands. "Please take that."

"Where to?"

"The furthest end of the clearing."

He snorted. "Are you trying to get rid of me?"

"Yes."

"I was just being helpful."

"You'd be a whole lot more helpful if you stuck that in the ground—" I pointed to the far end of the field. "—over there."

He walked off with a pout—which was just as cute as his smirk—and when he was out of earshot, I let out a sigh.

What had gotten into him?

He was full of innuendos and insinuations. He'd asked me if I'd slept in the same bed as a man before. He wanted me to take my shirt off. He wanted to rub sunscreen on my body . . .

Oh god. Was he actually flirting?

For real?

I watched him walking off to the far end of the field. His broad shoulders, his longish blondish-brown hair, his muscular legs.

No, he wasn't my usual type.

But damn, he could be . . .

"Is this far enough?" he yelled.

He'd gone about 75% of the distance but it didn't matter. I only needed a moment without him near me to try and clear my head. I gave him a thumbs-up and got busy setting up my laptop. The satellite radar was lagging, blinking in and out. "Dammit."

"Oh, I can tell ya when it'll hit and how big she'll be," Tully said, walking back. That annoying not-annoying annoying grin in place.

I squinted at him. "What?"

"The storm," he said. Then he pointed skyward, over the line of trees in the direction we'd come. "Don't need no radar for that. Can't you feel the drop in pressure?"

I took stock of myself. "I, uh . . . I was busy."

I was busy thinking about you.

Tully reached into the back of the Jeep. "Help me pull the canopy on."

I closed the laptop and helped him lift the roof on and clamp it into place, which he did with considerably more ease than me. By the time I was done, he'd packed up my crate and put it in the back. "Come on, we'll drive up to the other end so we can watch her come in. She's blowin' in from the east, pushed back by the warm air from the ocean up north. And you know what that means . . . ?"

"Well, I know what it means when cold air meets warm air in a low-pressure front," I said. "But in relation to your directional points of east and north, given I'm not from here, I'm not too familiar."

He laughed, and after we passed the tripod he'd stuck into the ground, he pulled the Jeep to a stop. "Storms from the east tend to get a little wild."

A thrill buzzed through me. Not just from his stupid smile and the spark in his eyes, but from the mention of a wild storm.

Just then the wind picked up, making us both turn in the direction we'd come. And sure enough, above the tree line, due east, was a front of clouds. Dark, bubbling, and brewing, with gentle intra-cloud sparkles of lightning, as if someone had filled a jar with black cotton balls and fairy lights.

"It's beautiful," I said.

The skies replied with a crack of thunder so loud, so close, it felt like a physical blow.

"Jesus!" Tully cried, ducking down.

I laughed and got out of the Jeep to set the camera up.

Hell yes. This is what I was here for. This—the thrill of a storm, the rush, the elements so close you could almost touch them.

I could definitely smell it. I could taste the ozone, the copper on my tongue.

It was so close.

More thunder boomed and lightning crackled along veins in the clouds, and I hurried to make sure he'd anchored the tripod properly, to make sure the camera was facing the right way.

The anemometer was spinning faster now, the wind tousling my hair. "Open my laptop," I yelled out to Tully. But I looked back to see he already had it open on the dash of the Jeep. I liked that he knew what to do, that he was as into this as me . . .

Lightning cracked with a boom of thunder right at the front of the clearing.

"Holy shit! Did you get that?"

"Yes!" I wasn't sure how, given the thrill, the pure adrenaline rush, was making my hands shake.

The skies were dark as the storm rolled toward us, a curtain front of rain marching through the clearing like an armoured battalion.

Another crack of lightning split the sky.

"Get in the fucking car!" Tully yelled. "Jeremiah, now!"

Like it was all the warning I needed, I made it into the passenger seat just before the wall of water rolled across us. Wind howled, tousling everything around us. Thunder rumbled constantly, low and threatening, with the occasional booms for emphasis. Lightning danced above us, around us, in an amazing display of power. Intra-cloud, cloud-to-ground, sheet lightning illuminating the otherwise darkened sky.

Tully peered out over the steering wheel, looking up and out. The flashes of lightning a strobe effect in the Jeep, showing me flashes of his face, of his smile, of the look of wonder. How he laughed every time lightning jittered through the clouds, through the sky.

It made my heart race for a whole other reason.

Maybe it was the storm. Maybe it was the thrill, the adrenaline, the power of it all, and maybe it was because I was experiencing it with him . . .

I was beginning to think I didn't need an internal warning system to know I could be in trouble.

I think I already knew.

CHAPTER SEVEN

TULLY

IT WAS GETTING ON DARK BY THE TIME WE GOT back to camp. Jeremiah went straight to work, plugging in his laptop and seeing what data he'd collected.

The storm had been a good one, and I was glad we'd made the effort to go stand in its path.

But something was different about Jeremiah. During the storm and after it.

Getting to sit with him in the Jeep, in such a confined space, while the storm put on a helluva show was insightful to say the least. Something about him changed when there was lightning. It wasn't excitement or exhilaration like I'd have thought. It wasn't some studious don't-miss-any-data attitude either.

There was a calmness to him. Serenity, almost. Like he was tryin' to drink it in through his skin.

He checked his smart watch, writing down all kinds of things in a notebook, separate from his laptop data. I'd noticed him doing that after last night's storm too but hadn't thought much of it.

"Whatcha writing down?"

He glanced up at me, the pen in his hand forgotten. "Oh, this . . . this is just for me. It's not really work, as such."

I looked at his watch. "Do you measure your vitals during a storm?"

He opened his mouth, then closed it and raised his chin. "It's just for me. My data, not for the bureau or for any public record. I'm just interested to know, as a side note. That's all."

"That's totally cool," I said, unsure as to why he was so guarded about it. "You said before you were interested to know what it did to the human body. Writing that shit down isn't a big surprise."

"Yes, well," he said, putting his pen down and closing his notebook. "Some people think it's stupid and that it undermines our actual research."

Ah. Clearly a co-worker or colleague with a superiority complex.

"Oh, fuck whoever said that," I said. "There are no rules to what you find fascinating. Only gatekeepers."

His gaze darted to mine. So fucking blue.

"Well, yes. Gatekeepers who keep me on the payroll."

"Oh. *Those* kind of gatekeepers."

He chuckled. "Yes, the one and the same."

"Well, stuck-up bosses aside, what you research on your own time has nothing to do with them. It's just very convenient, and maybe a little coincidental, that you can collate your personal data at the same time you collate theirs."

His smile lingered and died, the same way a sunset fades; beautiful and slow, the light giving way to the dark.

"I'm not particularly popular at work," he said quietly. "They all think I'm a little . . . weird. I believe creepy was the word used in an evaluation once."

"Creepy? What the fuck? You're not creepy."

His eyebrow flicked upward in a telling sign that he didn't agree with me. Or that others wouldn't, at least. "I learned a valuable lesson though," he said. "Not to disclose my personal interests in our field of study, and not to disclose sexual orientation in our field of study. I've been without a field partner ever since. So, what I learned is basically just do the work they pay me to do and shut up."

I frowned and sat on the bed with a heavy sigh. "Well, I'm sorry that happened. And also, fuck them. On both counts. Your reasons for studying meteorology and lightning are your own. Everyone has different reasons for doing whatever they do. And about the other thing . . . well, it ain't anyone's business who you take home." Then, for a joke, I added, "Unless you were banging someone in the office on company time."

I laughed, because it *was* a joke, but then he shot me a look that said . . .

"Oh shit, no way!" I barked out a laugh. "You banged someone in the office?"

His cheeks went red and he mumbled something to his notebook.

"What was that?" I asked. "I didn't quite catch it."

"It wasn't at work," he said indignantly. "It was someone at a meteorology convention, which was technically work time." The corner of his mouth pulled down. "At the convention, in a bathroom stall in the men's room."

I laughed for a solid two minutes. "Holy shit, Jeremiah, you sly dog! That's awesome." I studied him, his nerdy, sexy self, with the ripped body and giant doctor brain. "I gotta say, I'm proud. And a little jealous."

His gaze shot to mine. "Jealous. Of whom?"

I snorted. Of whom? *Whooom.* Who the hell said whom?

"Jealous that you got your freak on at a work thing. In the bathroom stalls. Jealous that you've done that and I haven't." I shrugged without a skerrick of shame. "And jealous of the guy you were in there with. Because damn, Jeremiah, that's hot as fuck."

His cheeks turned an incredible pink, and so did the tips of his ears. He cleared his throat. "Yes well, my boss didn't think so. I managed to come out of the stall and come out of the closet all at the same time. My boss and two other state managers were at the sink, washing their hands."

I laughed again, holding my stomach. "That's the best story I've ever heard. Why didn'tcha have an exiting-the-stall strategy?"

He stared at me. "Strategy? We didn't even have an entering-the-stall strategy. We made eye contact at the bar, I needed to use the bathroom, he followed me. I'm still not sure how it happened."

I laughed again, this time clutching his pillow. "God, that makes it so much better."

"I fail to see how."

"Did you ever see him again?"

"Once, at the same convention the following year. I avoided all eye contact, should he assume it was another invitation. I didn't want to get fired."

"That's perfect."

He sighed and pushed his notebook closer to his laptop. "I received a disciplinary caution."

I laughed again. "Totally worth it."

And right there was the flicker of a smile. But he chose to say nothing.

After a moment of silence, I nodded to his notebook. "So, what do you write down? Just info from your watch, like heart rate and stuff?"

He paused, like he was weighing up whether or not to tell me. "Yes. It monitors heart rate, like most smart watches, I would guess. It's not the expensive kind, but I also have an app that goes further."

"Ooh, that's cool. Like what?"

"Electrical pulses," he answered, kinda cryptically. "But it's not calibrated, and I can't use it as actual theory because it's not certified. It's just my curiosity."

"The effects lightning has on the human body."

His blue eyes bore into mine. "Yes."

"We should get one of those things that athletes use. You know how they tie those bands around their chests? We could totally hook you up and run real tests. There has to be doctors that do this shit." Then I winced. "I mean, medical doctors." Then I winced harder. "Sorry."

He rolled his eyes. "There are."

"And?"

"They can't condone my experiments because of the risk."

"But you're a fulminologist," I countered. "The risk is implied. That'd be like a doctor not listening to a pilot about the effects of a pressurised cabin on long-haul flights."

He smiled. "I take the data anyway. For my own satisfaction."

"Well, I think that's cool as hell."

He smiled. A real smile this time. "Thank you."

"And I'm serious about the heart-monitor thing." Because that was interesting, and it was cool. "We should totally do that."

"I'd like to take blood tests," he added. "And I'd like to do an electrical pulse study on the brain while standing under a lightning storm."

Aaaand we took a little sideways step from cool into weird territory. "Um. Why?"

His face flinched, then smoothed out as he collected himself. His demeanour changed. He raised his chin. "To study the effects of lightning on the human body."

I shook my head. "No, why do you really want to do it? Not just a blanket response that you've practiced for your stuck-up colleagues. Why? The real reason."

"Because the human body runs on electrical impulses. The brain, the heart, every cell. It *has* to affect us more than we currently believe."

"But doctors have studied people who've been struck by lightning," I said. "They have heart problems, organ problems, blindness, deafness."

"I'm aware of that, yes."

"Do you think people gain superpowers?" I asked, joking. "Like Thor?"

He didn't think that was funny. He scowled at me.

I studied him, his guarded face. "What else are you looking for, Jeremiah? You gotta have something you think is there." Then it dawned on me. "You're looking for proof."

He flinched. "I'm not *looking* for proof. I *am* proof."

I turned his words over in my head.

I am proof.

Jesus Christ.

"You've been struck by lightning?"

Those blue eyes lasered into me, sapphire fire, before he looked away. "Indirectly. But yes."

God.

"When?"

"I was two years old."

"Oh my god. How . . . what the fuck? Jeremiah, my god, what happened?"

He was quiet for a long few seconds, the sounds of the night loud in the silence. Crickets, cicadas, birds, the wind, all urging him to speak.

"I was in a stroller," he murmured. "My mother was pushing me. It was a freak afternoon storm in the city. She was running for the tram in the rain when lightning struck the tram line. Her foot was on the track . . ."

Holy shit.

Holy fucking shit.

I could see the image in my head, and the footage, because I'd seen it. The whole country had. It was caught on a security camera in Collins Street, Melbourne. All those years ago. I remembered this story . . . I remembered how the lightning flashed, sparks flew out of the tram wires, and a woman on the road was struck, her body flung side to side as if she'd been shot, her stroller slowly rolling away.

That footage was still famous. It was still replayed, still used to propagate storm safety messages to this very day.

Christ all-fucking-Mighty.

"That was you?"

With his back to me now, his shoulders sagged, and he gave a nod.

"God, Jeremiah, I'm so sorry."

"They said I wasn't harmed because the stroller had rubber wheels," he said, his voice detached and quiet. "I was two. I can't possibly remember it, so perhaps it was the footage." He turned to me then. "Maybe seeing the footage over and over has implanted false memories in my mind, or my imagination. I don't know. It's weird because the footage is from a different angle to my memories, so I can't be sure. I assume you've seen it?"

I nodded. "On Collins Street."

"I can remember my mother's face when she was struck. Just a fleeting moment of surprise before she spun away." He shrugged. "In my memory, it's not raining. But in the footage, it's pouring. And in my memory, I'm facing her but in the footage I'm not. So I can only assume it's all just false memories. Put there by the photographs my father has, and that damn footage."

I went over to him and put my hand on his arm. "I'm really sorry."

"My entire life has been shaped by lightning."

"It's why you're so driven to understand it. That makes sense. I'd want to understand it too."

He inhaled deeply and let it out on a sigh. "The doctors said I was very lucky. The blowback and side-flash hit me, but I was unharmed. More or less. But what it did to my mother . . ."

I didn't remember any of the gruesome details. Maybe they were disclosed at the time but not later. In the footage, afterward, it just showed her body covered with a sheet.

"Jeremiah," I whispered, sliding my hand up to his shoulder and giving it a squeeze. "You don't need to explain anything to me. The dipshits you work with might think you're creepy for trying to learn more, but if anything, I think I understand you better now. How could you not want to know?"

His eyes searched mine, maybe looking for sincerity. I hoped he found it. I was dead serious. "If you want help trying to learn more, I'll help you," I offered. "It's fascinating as hell to me."

The corner of his mouth lifted just a fraction. "You don't think I'm crazy? The weirdo lightning guy?"

"If you're the weirdo lightning guy, then I'm the weirdo storm-chaser guy. Everyone I know thinks I've got some roos loose in the top paddock, if you know what I mean."

He smiled then. "Thanks."

"I mean, we have to be a little bit unhinged to do what we do," I relented. "But, on the bright side, the fact we know this is just a little insane proves we're not actually crazy, right?"

"Right."

"I mean, you don't want to actually wrap yourself in tin

foil and go stand out in a lightning storm, so I think we're well ahead of the insanity crowd."

He chuckled and sighed. "If I ever get the urge, I'll let you know."

"Solid plan." I gave his shoulder a little shake. "Okay, so now we've got all that out of the way, tell me what you write in your little secret notebook. Let's look at your data."

CHAPTER EIGHT

JEREMIAH

TULLY DIDN'T RIDICULE ME. IN FACT, HE WAS interested in my findings and wanted further analysis. He made me help him cook dinner, and he asked all kinds of questions.

He knew about my mother and didn't ask me insensitive questions. In fact, he asked me no questions at all on that whole subject, and I was glad. He said he'd seen the footage—almost everyone on the planet had—and maybe that was all he needed to know.

It made me like him even more.

Not to mention that I'd openly discussed being caught having 'private interactions' with a male colleague, and he didn't even bat an eyelid. In fact, he'd found it hilarious. We'd skirted around the 'sleeping with a man in your bed before' conversation, which he'd freely admitted he had.

But I'd known Tully Larson for all of three days, and he knew my deepest, darkest secrets. No one in my real life knew these things about me after three days, some never at all. But it was so easy to talk to him.

Maybe because this was only temporary.

Maybe because when this was over and I went back to Melbourne, I'd never see him again.

Divulging secrets to strangers was so much easier.

I felt freer than I had in a long time. I was my true and honest self with him, and that told me more about my relationship with Tully than any analysis could.

I trusted him.

And I trusted very few people.

Even getting into bed with him was different this night. There was no awkwardness, no shyness. There was still shirtlessness, on his behalf, and I was still not opposed.

He was incredibly sexy.

And he was incredibly inquisitive. He hadn't stopped asking questions yet.

The lights were out, the netting on the bed was down, and I'd just laid down with the sheet up to my waist.

He was sat on the bed, legs half crossed, his knee almost touching me. He wore nothing but loose-fitting sleep shorts that revealed a little too much and nowhere near enough. "So, if we got one of those ECG reader things that the athletes wear around their chests," he said, "we can get better readings. Is there some kind of brain reader thing that's portable? I'll be the guinea pig if you want. Stick those circle pad things to my noggin and see what happens."

"You do remember that we're currently in the middle of nowhere, yes? Where do you propose we get such instruments?"

He made a face. "Well, I'm just thinkin' out loud. If you really wanted to, we could pack up and drive back to

Darwin. It'd only take us a day or two and we could come back."

I smiled at his enthusiasm. "I think the heart rate data from my watch will suffice for now, but thanks."

"Well, next time you come out, we'll have the proper gear, and we can do it then."

"Next time?" As much as I liked the sound of that, it wasn't likely. "I highly doubt my department will approve another grant for me to come up here."

"You get holidays though, right? Like four weeks a year?"

"Well, yes, but . . ."

"But what?"

"But I don't exactly have the funds to do this again. I don't . . ." I sighed. "I don't earn a great wage."

He frowned, a sad pout, then he shrugged. "You'd just need the airfares. I got the rest. I'm coming out here anyway. It's no extra cost to have you here. The food, the fuel, the water, I gotta bring all that whether you're here or not."

I wasn't sure what to say to that. The offer, the invite, was very generous. Very kind, if not a little premature.

He laid down with a huff. "If you don't wanna, that's fine. It's just been kinda nice to have some company. Especially someone who likes storms as much as I do. I'm normally out here for a week or two on my own, which is how I've always liked it. I brought my brother once, and I wanted to kill him by day two. First and last time for that, lemme tell ya."

I snorted. "You could have thrown his body in the river with the crocs. No one would have ever known."

He nudged me with his elbow. "I told him that! But he didn't think it was funny and he made me drive him home. He told Mum and Dad what I said."

I laughed, and the warm rumble of his laughter filled something inside me. "I'd like to come back," I admitted. "It's not that I don't want to, it's just that . . . you know. Money."

"Hm." I felt him shrug. "'S okay."

"I'll be paying off my uni debts forever," I mumbled.

"You did a lot of years, right? To be a doctor?"

"To earn my doctorate," I amended gently. "Yes. I did get a partial scholarship for the first four years. There were bursaries and stuff later on, but it was hard. My dad never understood why I chose meteorology and fulminology. I mean, he knows why, obviously. But he didn't agree with it. He thinks I'm trying to bring my mother back or some-thing. Like what I'm studying will honour her memory, but that's not why I chose it. It's not why I do it."

"You do it because it changed your life. That day when you were two. It put you on a certain path."

I nodded, my heart blooming with the warmth that he understood. "Exactly. And we never had much money. Dad did what he could do, but his life changed forever that day too and certainly not for the better. I think he resents lightning. He hates it. And I understand that," I admitted. "He said if I'm so smart, I should have used my brains to be a real doctor or an engineer or something that earned a lot of money. He doesn't understand why I'd want to choose to be broke my whole life when I had the option not to be."

Tully rolled onto his side, his head propped up on his

hand. He was close, we were sharing a small double bed after all, and his face looked a silvery blue in the dark. "Parents just want what they think is best for us. But that's not who you are," he said. "And you should be proud that you followed your heart. Not many have the courage to do that. They fall for the pressure to do what they're supposed to do. Like me, I work in a family business that I have no real interest in. But it's a cushy job and it pays well—well, they pay good money because I'm family. I'm good at my job, get shit done, produce the numbers that make people happy, and I'm told I'm very good at it. But I don't love my job. I don't live for it. My eldest brother and my sister, they love what they do. They live and breathe that shit, and it makes them happy, so good for them. But to me, it's just a job."

"A job that gives you time off during the storm season to camp out here for weeks on end."

He grinned, his teeth white in the dark. "Exactly."

Then something between us shifted. The air, the pressure, the electrical charge between us, and it had nothing to do with the weather.

He stared at me, and I couldn't look away. His gaze felt like lasers burning everything in their wake. He licked his lips and I gasped, or moaned, or . . . leaned in. Or maybe it was him leaning in. The dark was disorienting, or maybe it was the fact I hadn't breathed in a minute or two . . .

Then he blinked and pulled back, shaking his head a little. "Oh wow, yeah, okay," he said, falling down onto his back with a huff. "That probably shouldn't happen." He turned his head to look at me. "Your eyes are really fucking blue and I feel like I'm falling into water or some shit."

I had to put my hand on my chest to try and calm my hammering heart. "Ah, yeah, I hear that a lot." I shook my head. "Not about the falling into water thing. That's new. But yes, blue."

"But they're a weird blue. Like freakishly blue. Is that from the lightning?"

I scoffed. "What?"

"Like a superpower from being struck by lightning. Are you secretly an X-Men member? Can you shoot laser beams out of your eyes?"

I sighed but was glad he was joking. I thought he might have been serious . . . "Pretty sure that's Cyclops, and no, I'm not him. Or any member of the X-Men."

"Shame."

"Yeah, not really."

He chuckled. "So I almost kissed you before," he said with a sigh, as if he was discussing something completely mundane. "Just in case you weren't aware."

My pulse was thumping, my heart in my throat. I had to swallow so I could speak. "Uh, I might have picked up on that."

"But it's not something we've discussed, and I personally happen to find consent extremely sexy."

My pulse was now staccato.

"Almost as sexy as you," he added, so very nonchalantly. He could have been discussing his favourite kind of toothpaste. He sighed again. "Almost. I mean, you do have a rockin' hot body under all that science nerd."

My watch beeped.

Traitorous piece of technology . . .

"What's that alarm for?" Tully asked, grabbing my wrist. I tried to pull my hand away, but he lifted it up so he could read the screen. "What does that mean?"

"Nothing," I blurted out.

"It says you should take a rest. But you're not doing anything."

"It must need resetting," I said, pulling my arm from his grasp. I fumbled with the watchband.

Tully laughed, rolling onto his side, somehow closer now. His chest touched my arm, his face so close to mine. Too close to mine. He smiled and pulled his bottom lip in between his teeth.

My watch beeped again before I managed to rip it off.

"Is your watch telling me something?" he asked.

"I hate your stupid smile," I said, dumping my watch onto the floor beside the bed.

Tully laughed, a warm, rumbly sound that was far too close. "If your heart rate's up, you're either excited or terrified. Which is it?"

Both.

"Neither."

He dragged his index finger up my chest, stopping at the base of my throat. "I don't believe you. But—" He rolled back onto his back with a huff. "—like I said, consent is my foreplay. No green light, no go."

My heart was knocking so hard against my ribs it hurt, and I had to pretend I could breathe normally. But I couldn't speak.

He rolled onto his other side, facing away. "Night, Jeremiah."

I wanted to tell him yes. I wanted to reach out and touch him, bring him back to where he'd been when he was so close I could feel his body heat.

But I still couldn't form the words, and then I left it too long to say anything.

Not even goodnight.

———

TULLY WAS UP and out of bed when I woke. I wasn't surprised, but it did sting. I didn't want things to be awkward between us.

I didn't know what I wanted between us.

A quick fling? A sex-buddy for my stay?

It certainly wouldn't be hurting anyone.

Unless he had someone at home who would be hurt ...

I sat up on the bed, my feet on the floor and scratched my head. Tully was walking back across the clearing, swatting away a fly. Shirtless, his skin radiant in the early morning sun with a sheen of sweat ...

My cock certainly liked it, not helped by the fact I needed to pee. I made a dash for the bathroom before he got any closer so he couldn't see the tent in my boxers, but I didn't want him to think I was hiding from him.

"Morning," I called out before I closed the bathroom door.

"Oh, sleeping beauty has arisen," he said. "Want some breakfast?"

"Ah, sure."

Glad that things seemed to be normal between us, I

took a real quick shower and brushed my teeth. And as I was drying off and pulled on my shorts, I had a thought.

I wanted him to know I was okay with what he'd said last night. And actually, I appreciated his asking. He could have just kissed me, and truthfully, I'd have let him. God, last night I'd have let him do whatever he wanted to me. But he wanted to ask first. He needed to know if I was on board, giving me full control.

And I liked that a lot.

I respected that.

It made me want to say yes. Which brought up a whole new set of problems because it was unlikely he'd ask a second time, so it was now up to me to make the first move.

If I wanted something to happen between us . . .

Which I did.

Well, my libido did. My dick was half-hard again at the thought of it; the cold shower clearly hadn't been cold enough.

So how the hell did I go about this?

With my shirt in my hand, I looked down at myself. He did say he wouldn't mind if I went shirtless, and it was hot today already . . .

So, before I lost my nerve, I walked out of the bathroom and tossed my shirt onto my bag.

Tully had a frypan of scrambled eggs in his hand, but he was stuck, staring at me with his mouth open.

I tried not to smile as I put my watch back on. "You're about to lose your eggs."

He snapped his mouth shut and righted the frypan.

"Oh, I see the game you're playing, mister sexy science guy."

I looked down at my stomach and ran my hands over my abs and over my pec. "What? It's hot as hell today."

"It just got a whole lot hotter."

I snorted, secretly pleased at his reaction. "You don't wear a shirt, and you said I could do the same."

"I'd also tell you you don't have to wear shorts but I'm pretty sure I wouldn't handle that." He looked down to my crotch. "I mean, you're almost not wearing those as it is."

"What do you mean?"

"They're so low slung I know exactly where your happy trail goes."

I gasped and pulled my shorts up. "They're just old. The elastic isn't great."

And the material was a little thin now. Okay, perhaps a *lot* thin because Tully was still staring at them.

"Were you wearing those when that guy followed you into the bathroom stall? Because honestly, I can see why he couldn't resist."

I folded the waistband over to try and keep them up.

He put the fry pan down on the stove and stared at my crotch. "Jesus fucking Christ, are you goin' commando right now?"

I covered my dick with my hands. "What are you looking for?"

He spun around so he wasn't looking, his hands on his head. "Are you *trying* to kill me?"

"I don't like underwear," I said. "I never wore them much growing up, and I find they ride up . . ." I huffed. "If we could stop talking about my genitals, that'd be great."

He whipped his head around, his eyes shot to mine. "It ain't my fault you came out here naked."

"I'm not naked!"

"You might as well be."

"I can change my shorts to something more appropriate, if you'd prefer."

"I would *not* prefer that." He waved his hand up and down at me. "I prefer this, thank you very much. Just warn a guy next time."

I felt bad now and terribly self-conscious. My plan to perhaps entice him a little had well and truly overshot the runway. I went to my bag, picked up my shirt and quickly pulled it on.

"Aww," Tully cried. "You can't show me an unwrapped present then re-wrap it. That's not how this works. Leave the shirt off."

I shook my head and, hoping to move on from this embarrassing conversation, took two plates out. "Sorry. Want me to help serve the eggs? They look good."

He scowled at me. "T-shirt, one-star rating. Do not recommend." Then he looked down at my shorts. "Shorts, on the other hand, five stars. Highly recommended. Actually, the fact the shirt now hides the front of the shorts makes the shirt negative stars."

"Negative stars isn't a thing."

He raised one eyebrow, his gaze raking down to my crotch and back up to my eyes. "Oh, I assure you, it is."

I took the frypan from in front of him and dished up the eggs. "Thank you for cooking breakfast."

He pouted. "I'm still sad."

I rolled my eyes and laughed, glad that all awkwardness was gone. I cleaned up after breakfast, and we set about doing some work.

It was so unbearably hot and so humid, by two o'clock, I couldn't stand it. I pulled off my shirt and wiped the sweat off my face and chest with it. When I looked at Tully, he was grinning at me like a kid on Christmas morning.

"Shut up," I grumbled. "It's too bloody hot."

He ogled me, deliberately, from head to foot and back up again, stopping midway and shaking his head. "And it's getting hotter by the second." He shrugged with no shame. "I'm not joking, the temperature is actually rising." He turned the laptop to face me. "And the humidity's gonna get to a breaking point before the hour's out. This storm right here." He pointed to the large band of red and purple. "She's gonna be a good one."

I found myself smiling at him. "Excellent. I better get my gear set up." I went to my bag and rummaged around for the sunscreen and rubbed some into my face and chest. It might have been cruel and it was probably uncalled for, but I handed the tube to him and turned around, speaking to him over my shoulder. "Can you rub some in for me, please?"

He huffed with fake annoyance. Or maybe it was real, I wasn't sure. "If I have to. I mean, now you're givin' me an unwrapped present, you're lettin' me touch it," he said, smearing sunscreen across my shoulder and rubbing it in with strong, firm strokes. "But I still can't play with it."

My heart skidded and my belly swooped. Then my fucking watch beeped again, and he laughed. He was so close his breath was warm on my skin, his hands now rubbing sunscreen down my spine.

"You can pretend all you like," he whispered. "But your heart rate doesn't lie."

"The app must be glitching," I said, and maybe that would have been convincing if my voice hadn't come out all rough.

He chuckled behind me, his hands now running down my sides, fingertips digging in.

Not wearing underpants today had been a big mistake.

I cleared my throat and took a step forward, away from him. I half turned, not letting him see the tented commando issue I had going on at the front. "Thank you," I said, then walked out into the blistering sun and the suffocating humidity.

Thirty seconds of that torture and I no longer had a hard-on. Small mercies, I guess.

I checked the automatic weather station in the clearing, making sure everything was still intact and working, then looked up at the gathering clouds. There was a front coming in from the east again; a dark and foreboding wall of mother nature was coming our way.

It felt like the air would catch fire before it rained. As if one spark of lightning could light the whole sky up like a match to gasoline.

I went back to the shed, amazed at the difference in temperature inside. "How freaking hot is it out there? The tropics are brutal."

Tully didn't seem too fazed. "You get used to it." Then he nodded to my crotch and shrugged. "But you could take your shorts off if you get too hot."

I resisted rolling my eyes.

But then he was serious. He came over with a bottle of water and pressed it to my sternum. "Keep drinking water and take cool showers if you feel like you're over-heating." And then he was back to being Tully; he stared at my chest and abs and shook his head. "Damn, Jeremiah. How do you do it? What's your routine?"

"My routine for what?"

"In the gym."

"I don't go to the gym." I made a face. "Where there are other people, all sweaty and showing off. It's gross."

He gave me a crooked smile, and I was waiting for my watch to betray me, but thankfully it didn't. "So you work out at home?"

"I don't work out." Well, that wasn't exactly true. "I swim. For no other reason than it clears my head. And it's solitary. No one can speak to me while I do laps."

He laughed, his eyes alight with something I wasn't brave enough to name. "You crack me up."

"Glad I amuse you."

"Ah, don't be like that," he said, giving me a gentle nudge. "You are . . ." He met my gaze and shook his head. "Like no one I've ever met before."

"I can only assume that was because you don't frequent science conventions or libraries."

"Ouch."

I shrugged. It was true.

A bead of sweat chose that moment to run from my temple, down my jaw and neck, and of course he watched it, his eyes intense. So, meeting fire with fire, I opened the bottle of water, put it to my lips, and drank.

He watched my mouth and my throat as I swallowed, his eyes dark, his lips parted.

I wiped the back of my hand across my mouth to hide my smile and offered him the bottle. "Some?"

His nostrils flared. "You're a cruel man."

I grinned at him. "I don't know what you're talking about. If you don't want the water, just say no."

He narrowed his eyes at me and snatched the bottle, then took a step back before he turned and walked away. "Christ, it's hot in here."

I pressed my lips together so as not to smile too wide. This was kinda fun. I knew how it would end; it was why I was doing it. I hadn't come here expecting any such thing —it was the last thing I expected, truthfully—but now it was a possibility?

Ending with a romp on that small double bed with a gorgeous man wouldn't be terrible. If he was willing . . .

And he *was* willing.

Then I remembered something. Before I took this any further . . .

I went to my laptop, tracking the storm, pretending to be grossly interested in it. "So," I hedged, trying for the nonchalance that he did so well. "Anyone in Darwin on your emergency contact list I should know about?"

He squinted at me, confused. "Emergency contact?" Then he came to see the radar. "Just how bad is this storm gonna get?"

"No, it's not that bad. I mean, it's a good one. There's a wind warning in conjunction with high precipitation falls and a flash flood warning for some parts. Decent lightning activity."

Tully looked at me then. "Why did you ask about my emergency contact? That's a random and totally weird thing to ask, not gonna lie."

"No, it's not that, it's just . . ." I shook my head and looked out at the darkening sky instead. "It's just good to know if something were to happen, who I should call, that's all. Like someone who would be upset if you were injured."

"Oh my god," he whispered. Aaaaand then he grinned. "Are you tryin' to ask me if I'm seeing someone back home?"

My eyes shot to his.

He laughed. "You totally are!"

Thunder rolled outside.

"You wanna know if I'm seein' someone. That's what this is all about. You taking your shirt off. Asking me to rub sunscreen on your back. Drinkin' water like a porn star."

"I did not drink that water like a porn star."

"You did fucking so."

"Just what kind of porn do you watch?"

"Don't try and change the subject."

I had an all too familiar taste hit my mouth and I licked my lips, tried to swallow it down. "I need some water."

Suddenly serious, he handed me the bottle. "Why do you do that? You did it the other day too. Like something tastes bad before it rains."

I sipped the water, swishing it in my mouth even though I knew it wouldn't help. "Not before it rains. Before the lightning."

His eyes met mine. "What?"

"I know when lightning is about to strike," I said. "Because I can taste it."

"You can taste it," he whispered, not a question, but this was usually when people thought I was weird. Like he was now. I could see it on his face.

"It's a metallic taste. Copper, to be exact." I tried to swallow down the taste on my tongue, as if the mention of it made it worse. "It's not pleasant. But it's common," I said. "In people who've been struck by lightning."

His eyes searched mine and a slow smile spread across his face. Okay, so maybe he didn't think I was weird. "That is soooo fucking cool!"

CHAPTER NINE

TULLY

Thunder clapped right above us, scaring the shit out of me. "Jesus!" I ducked on instinct.

Jeremiah didn't even flinch.

He could taste lightning.

Well, not *actual* lightning. But he could taste when it was close.

That was the coolest thing I'd ever heard.

He really was like no one I'd ever met before.

And he was being all kinds of weird all day. After last night, I probably couldn't blame him. I did almost kiss him. Hell, lying in bed with him so close, and so freaking sexy, kissing him wasn't all I wanted to do.

But he didn't answer when I asked him, and anything short of a direct yes is a no.

So I'd rolled over and gone to sleep, disappointed but not mad about it.

Then today, he woke up with an agenda, clearly.

Maybe it was his way of answering me with a yes?

Trying to be all seductive and shit. First, being shirtless.

Then asking me to rub sunscreen in, which was as cliché as it was awesome. And the water bottle incident. Christ almighty.

He was playing a dangerous game.

And then—then!—he asked if I was seeing someone. Not outright, but that's what he was hinting at.

"I'm single," I said casually. "And considering I'm bisexual, you'd think I'd have double the options, but no. I'm doubly undatable, apparently."

He glanced up from his laptop, looked me up and down, and went back to the laptop. "I find that hard to believe."

"Why?"

He gestured to me, like that was his answer. "You look like the love child of Patrick Swayze and Chris Hemsworth."

I snorted. "I can't help that."

"Yes, because it would be so problematic." He rolled his eyes.

"What is problematic is that I spend my weekends camping out, and every holiday I get, I chase storms. I don't have commitment issues. I'm just committed to the wrong things. Apparently."

He smirked, still looking at the screen. "Sounds like you've heard that a few times."

"I have."

His blue eyes shot to mine. "Then you're dating the wrong people."

Oof.

Those eyes, and those words.

Damn.

"What about you? Seeing anyone? I probably should have asked you that before I almost kissed you last night. Though, broadly speaking, I did ask permission if I could kiss you so that covers that, right?"

His cheeks bloomed with blush. Or maybe it was the heat.

His watch beeped that warning sound. Ignoring it, he turned to his laptop instead. "Okay it's coming, we need to run the intra-cloud activity," he said.

"Is your watch working properly now? Or is it still glitching?"

He shot me a hard glare.

"Funny how it only glitches when I'm next to you," I said. "Almost like my presence makes your heart rate spike."

He stabbed some keys on his keyboard. "What's your reading?" he asked, ignoring my poke at him completely.

I looked at the screen, not sure what he wanted. I didn't know how to read any of this. "The amplitude pulses?"

"The spatiotemporal analysis of radiation field pulses," he mumbled, turning the screen to face him. His eyes scanned over the data and he nodded. "We should get some good readings." Then he did that mouth/tongue thing again, like something tasted bad.

And boom!

Thunder cracked right on top of us and lightning lit up the sky.

He really could taste it.

A huge gust of wind brought with it the smell of rain,

and then the clouds opened up, bucketing thick, heavy drops.

"Shit," I said, racing to close the side wall down. "The wind's bringing it in." Some of our gear got wet, bags and clothes, but we'd have to deal with that later. Jeremiah helped with the other side and we got the wall lowered, to stop the rain coming in sideways at least.

The wind roared around the shed, rain pelted down, thunder was a constant rumble and bang, and lightning cracked all around us.

Jeremiah ran back to his recording gear, then leaned in, squinting at the screen. "Shit," he said. "The anemometer must be down on the station."

Then, like an idiot with zero thought for self-preservation, he ducked out under the other side wall and disappeared into the storm.

"Are you crazy?" I yelled out after him, but it was no use. He was halfway across the clearing.

Thunder clapped hard, right above us, and a bolt of lightning struck ahead of us. Maybe a hundred metres in the trees. But that sonofabitch never stopped running. He didn't even flinch. Surely, he saw it. It was right fucking there! He just kept running right toward it.

"Jeremiah! The fuck are you doing?"

There was no point. There was no way he could hear me over the rain and the thunder.

He reached the tripod station, skidding to a stop. He grabbed the arms with the small wind cups and fixed it.

Yes, please run out into a lightning storm to wrap your hands around the metal instrument in the middle of a clearing.

It was like sending lightning a freaking invitation to strike him down.

The man was fucking insane.

He came running back, the wind was wild, spraying rain in all directions. A sonic crack of thunder with lightning that felt like a direct hit, lit up our entire camp.

I expected Jeremiah to get knocked off his feet. I expected him to get blowback, or a side blast. I expected to see him take a direct fucking hit.

But he didn't. He just kept running toward me, his hair plastered to his face, his entire body soaked.

And grinning.

He ducked under the side wall like in the movies where they run for a closing roller door. Just like that. And he clambered to his feet, panting and dripping water, and then that fucker laughed.

He laughed.

Whereas I, on the other hand, was really fucking pissed.

I shoved his chest. "Are you insane?"

His smile died. "What?"

I pointed to the outside. "Do you know how close that was? Do you know how fuckin' close that was? I'm glad you got that on video so I could have shown the coroner that you died for being a fucking idiot."

His chest was heaving, he was drenched from head to foot. His eyes narrowed at me. He grabbed my face, hard and rough, and for a second I thought he was going to hit me, or shove me backwards for calling him an idiot . . . but he pulled me toward him and crushed his mouth to mine. He held my face and plunged his tongue into my mouth, totally dominating. Totally fucking hot.

I took his tongue willingly and gave him mine. He sucked on it, then pulled my bottom lip in between his, kissing me one last time before pulling back. My god, he could kiss.

He grinned, lips red and swollen, still drenched from head to foot. "That was a rush."

It took my brain a second to catch up but I couldn't put words together. My head was still spinning while he was already at the table checking his screens for data. I put my hand to my forehead and focused on what he'd said. "What was a rush? The storm? Or the kiss?"

"The storm." He gave me a look that said, 'what kiss?' like he hadn't just had his tongue down my throat.

Like he hadn't just given me the best kiss of my life.

Something on the table beeped and he picked it up, then went to his laptop, double checking something . . . I don't fucking know. I was too busy watching rivulets of water run down his back, how his wet shorts clung to him.

Without underwear.

"Holy fuck," I breathed.

He didn't look up. He just pointed to something out of his reach. "Pass me the sensor detector."

It took me a few seconds to move. I went and handed it to him, and he just continued to read and correlate data like nothing had just happened. "We've got upper negative and a lower positive charge," he said, reading three radar screens at the same time.

Did I imagine him kissing me?

My lips were still tingling, my whole body was tingling,

my brain was still offline . . . oh yeah, he'd definitely kissed me. And now he stood there reading some machine, water puddling at his feet, dripping from his shorts . . . shorts that did nothing to hide the outline of his cock.

His long, half-hard and uncut cock.

Christ.

"Tully?"

My mind snapped back to reality, and I dragged my eyes up to meet his. "Huh?"

He smirked. That fucker smirked. "You zoned out on me. You okay?"

"Ah, not really," I said. "You kissed me. I had your tongue in my mouth not two minutes ago and now you're acting like nothing happened." I waved my hand at his body. "And those shorts, when wet, leave nothing to the imagination. Nothing. I don't know where you got them from, but they are absolutely a five-star purchase. Highly, *highly* recommended."

He stared at me.

"Are we not going to talk about you kissing me?" I asked.

He opened his mouth, then promptly shut it again, as if he was trying to remember if he'd kissed me or not. "I'm sorry. I was excited—I'd had a rush of adrenaline—and I apologise if it was out of line."

"Oh no," I said, shaking my head. "No apologies required. It was not out of line. It was very in of line. I don't know what the opposite of that is." I started again. "I was very okay with that. Where the fuck did you learn to kiss like that? Because Jesus, Mary, Joseph, and their freaking donkey, I ain't ever been kissed like that before.

And I'd like to add, the only thing you should apologise for is if you don't do it again."

He chewed on his bottom lip so he didn't smile too big.

"I would say don't get smug about it," I added, "but honestly, you should be. Full credit where credit is due. It's worthy of the all-kissing accolades. If they gave Nobel prizes for kissing . . ."

He smiled then and ran his hand through his wet hair, brushing it up off his forehead, and damn if that didn't make him ten times hotter.

"I'm not seeing anyone," he said, as if I hadn't just rambled like an idiot. "Eternally single, I'm afraid. Too nerdy, too weird. Too focused on my work. Too . . ." He squinted. "I can't remember what else he said, but you get the picture."

"Then you're dating the wrong guy."

His gaze met mine, intense and searching, before he went back to his laptop. "Yes, well . . . and about the shorts. I should probably change. I'm dripping water—"

"Oh no. The shorts stay. You can't wear anything else for the duration of your stay." I put my hand to my chest. "As your official guide, I must insist. For safety reasons. It's very important."

His gaze locked with mine and his smile was interrupted by him biting his bottom lip. "I should go check the auto-station," he said quietly. He took a step backward, and of course my eyes went straight to his dick.

Yep. Still there. Still perfectly outlined. Still mouthwatering . . .

But then he turned and ducked under the awning, walking out into the clearing. The trees were blowing in the wind, but the rain was gone. He put his arms out. "How can it still be so hot?" he yelled.

I didn't realise just how big I was smiling as I watched him until he came back with the control panel and I had to school my features.

He set the control panel down. "We got some great readings," he said.

"Should we rewatch the video?" I asked. "And see just how close you were to getting zapped by lightning."

He stood at the table, facing me. His hands by his sides, his torso dry now, his shorts . . . damn, I couldn't stop staring. I tried to look away, but then his hand interrupted my view when he gave his dick a squeeze.

"Were you never told it's rude to stare," he murmured, his voice low and husky.

I made myself look up at his face, and his eyes were full of fire. Full of want.

Oh, hell fucking yes.

I went to him, gripped his chin in between my thumb and forefinger. "I want to suck your cock. Tell me yes or no."

He licked his lips and smiled as if he had all the time in the world. As if this was his game, he held all the cards, and I didn't even know the rules.

He was in charge, and I was 100% okay with that.

He leaned in, his lips against mine, his eyes dark and intense.

"Yes."

CHAPTER TEN

JEREMIAH

I WASN'T NORMALLY SO BOSSY WHEN IT CAME TO sex. Well, not *this* bossy. But it felt good to be in control and Tully seemed to like it that way.

He went to his knees, slowly, kissing down my chest and stomach, below my navel. He slid my shorts down over my arse and they went surprisingly easy, given they were still wet. He hummed as he took me into his mouth. No preamble, no toying. Just instant wet heat, sucking me, tonguing and moaning.

"Oh god," I mumbled, trying to rein in the pleasure. I fisted his hair, but it only seemed to spur him on.

Of course, he likes his hair pulled.

Fuck.

His hands clawed the backs of my thighs and my arse as he took me into his throat, swallowing around me.

God, I hadn't had this in so long, and he was doing everything so, so right.

I pulled his head back by his hair, making him look up at me, the head of my cock still in his mouth.

"So good," I mumbled, the coil of my orgasm needing to unwind so badly.

Then he cupped my balls and took me back in, sucking hard and pumping the base of my shaft.

"Oh fuck. Tully, I'm gonna come."

He smiled around my cock and hummed, and that was all it took.

Pleasure so complete detonated in my belly, my cock surged, and I came. He moaned as he drank me down and the room spun and my vision swam.

Tully sat me in a seat from the table, my senses still obliterated. My body was heavy, my mind was floating.

He lifted my chin, a smug smile on his face. "You okay there?"

"Hmm."

He straddled my legs and adjusted his erection, right in front of my face. "Yes or no?"

I pulled him closer by the waistband of his shorts, unbuttoning them. "Hell yes," I said, smiling. I pulled out his cock, thick and cut, and licked my lips before licking his slit.

"Oh fuck, I'm not gonna last long," he breathed.

I took him into my mouth, swirling my tongue around his shaft, flicking his frenulum. He shuffled closer as I took him deeper, and he made a high keening sound, pained almost.

"Fuck, Jeremiah," he rasped out.

Then his fingers slid around my jaw, my neck, and I could tell he was trying hard not to thrust in. He was so hard, so ready. I took him into my throat and he grunted and groaned, his cock swelling and shooting come down my throat.

I held his arse, keeping him buried in my throat until his body stopped twitching, and when I let him out, I pulled up his shorts, led him to the bed, and pushed him back onto it.

He landed with a gruff laugh. "Fuck yes," he said. He had his eyes closed and his lips curled in a serene smile. "Christ, you have skills. Kissing. Sucking dick. God. Did you study that?"

I snorted out a laugh and fixed my shorts. Then, not entirely sure what to do next, I grabbed my iPad. He raised his head off the bed. "Where are you going?"

"Nowhere." I came back to the bed and lay down beside him. "I'm gonna watch this."

I rewound the video and we lay there, both still shirtless, both now very sated, and we watched a replay of the storm. We could see the dark clouds rolling in, the wall of water as it came toward the bunker. I watched the sheet lightning light up the clouds like it was full of fireflies, mesmerised by how beautiful it could be.

Sparks of intra-cloud lightning shot across the clouds like spidery fingers, positive seeking out the closest source of negative charge. After a few minutes of raging winds, the auto-station fell over at the end of the clearing.

"Oh, here goes the crazy man," Tully said, "running out into a lightning storm to hold a metal rod."

Tully's voice in the video yelled at me too, and it was oddly comforting. That he should care enough to be concerned.

Just as I'd righted the anemometer, a bolt of lightning

cracked into the trees behind me, and I hit pause on the screen.

"Can you see why I was pissed?" Tully said. He rolled onto his side, hooking his foot over mine, locking me in some wrestling leg-manoeuvre. He pointed to the screen. "Look at how close that is. Look!"

"I can see," I said.

"You didn't even flinch or duck," he said.

But I wasn't looking at how close the strike was. I was looking at the pure energy, the brilliance of light. The raw power.

"It's perfect."

Tully rolled onto his back, letting my leg go with an exasperated sigh. "Yes, it's amazing. But can you appreciate that you almost died? And just wait till you get to the part where you slide in under the wall like an action movie hero." He sighed again. "I'm beginning to think you have the whole Clark Kent vibe going on."

I looked at him. "Clark Kent?"

"Yeah, sexy nerd front, kickass superhero when no one's looking."

I scoffed.

"He also risked his life unnecessarily all the time, too. Stupidly put himself in harm's way, as if his book-smarts mean diddley freakin' squat in the real world." Then he shrugged. "But totally gets his freak on in the bedroom. Can we talk about where you learned to kiss like that? And suck dick? Because that's some Kryptonite bullshit right there. Jesus."

I stared at him, not entirely sure if he was being serious. "No one taught me."

He grinned. So he was joking . . . "So you learned by yourself."

"By myself?" I squinted at him. "How could I possibly kiss myself? And I certainly can't suck my . . . self."

Now he laughed. "Have you tried?"

"No!" I barked, the silence that followed was loud. Then, because I had to ask . . . "My god, have you?"

"I'm not flexible enough to even try. But I've seen it in porn. It's kinda weird. Now, I love sucking dick, but my own? I think that'd be too weird, even for me."

I took a deep breath. "How is this even a conversation we're having?"

He rolled onto his side again, facing me with that unlawful smirk. He hooked his foot over mine again. "Because of the Clark Kent thing," he said casually. "And now that we've crossed the line once, I'd like to discuss the possibility of crossing it many times. So if there are any preferences or hard limits you'd like to discuss . . ."

It was difficult to think clearly when he was playing footsies and lying so close, and looking at me like that. With his smiling eyes and his perfect face.

"I'm here to work," I said, trying to relinquish some of the control he had over me. "And—"

"And work we will," he said, taking my iPad. "Later."

I took it back, scowling at him. "Trying to distract me with your charm and roguish good looks with the promise of more sex won't help your argument for being able to get work done and engage in some kind of sexual relationship."

He took the iPad again, this time leaning right over me and laying it on the floor beside the bed. This, of course, meant he was now kneeling over me, looking down at me. "Did you say roguish good looks?"

I rolled my eyes. "Your smile is ridiculous."

Laughing, he took hold of my leg and pulled me into the middle of the bed. "Glad you like it."

"I never said I liked it."

He leaned down, his nose almost touching mine. "Oh, but I think you do."

For some reason, it was getting harder to breathe. "At first I thought it made you likeable. Then it was annoying. Then it made me irrationally angry."

He licked his lips, smirking. "And now?"

My watch beeped.

"I hate it."

"No you don't." He laughed and took my wrist. "It says so right here. Though it didn't beep before when I sucked your dick. Was that not good for you?"

We both knew the answer to that.

I pulled my hand free and clawed at the stupid watch, trying to take it off. "I told you it glitched."

"Uh-uh." He gripped both of my hands and held them to the mattress above my head, making the watch beep again. Grinning now, he whispered against my lips. "Leave it on. It will tell me when I do something you like."

Oh god. My brain scrambled, making it difficult to think, to speak. "Scientifically speaking, heart acceleration is also frequent during moments of rage and fear," I said, my voice barely a whisper.

He ghosted his lips over mine. "Are you scared?"

My breath hitched.

"Are you angry?"

My traitorous hips tried to meet his, desperate for friction.

He grinned and crushed his mouth to mine, forcing his tongue inside. He still had my hands pinned to the bed and pressed his full weight between my legs, holding me down, kissing me hard. It was everything I wanted.

There was a beeping noise somewhere near my head, distant and hazy in the desire coursing through me, until it got louder and louder and louder . . .

My watch.

I groaned and pulled my hands free, ripping my watch off and tossing it somewhere near the iPad. "They're gonna send a rescue chopper if it doesn't stop," I said, then pulled his face back to mine.

He laughed into the kiss and rolled his hips, his erection rubbing against mine.

How was I hard again? How was he? Was it the heat? Or was it just him?

I think it was him.

He was so sexy, and he wanted me. Me.

Miserable, lonely, weirdo me.

He broke the kiss and groaned, rubbing and thrusting against me. "Oh god. Fuck, Jeremiah."

I slid my hand between us, fumbling to get our shorts down, to wrap my hand round us both.

His eyes shot open and he bucked, pressing his forehead to mine. "Holy shit."

Our cocks slid together, slick with our precome, mine, his.

He grunted, the noise setting every cell in my body on fire, and then he kissed me again, our tongues colliding.

And he shuddered, bucking, and with a loud cry, he came in my hand. His cock pulsing against mine, tripping me over the edge . . .

When the world stopped spinning, I opened my eyes to find him staring at me. "Holy shit," he breathed. "That was so fucking hot."

I couldn't speak.

I was so tired, and my bones were heavy and spongy. He collapsed on top of me, smearing the mess between us, and it was hot and we were both sweaty, and I didn't even care.

His breath was warm on my neck, and normally that would bother me.

But not with him.

Instead, I surrendered to the world, slung my arm around him, and closed my eyes.

I TOOK a mouthful of my dinner and scrolled the radar data. "Forecast for the next two days is good for lightning activity, but then two days of heavy precipitation. Up to one hundred millimetres."

Tully chewed thoughtfully and nodded. "We might have to pack up and leave before it hits."

My eyes shot to his, and I was struck by how much I didn't want that. "To higher ground? Or do you mean *leave* leave?"

He shoved in another forkful of rice and smiled as he chewed. "You sound disappointed."

"I am." I stabbed my rice, trying to play it cool. "I have

four more days here. It's highly unlikely I'll get this opportunity again. I need to collect adequate data to justify to my department the cost of my being here."

He did more of that smirking that I absolutely hated. "It has nothin' to do with your amazing guide who gives you mind-blowin' orgasms and cooks incredible dinners."

I frowned at him, unwilling to respond to the first part of his statement. "This rice is actually very good." It was a Thai-style fried rice with vegetables, spices, and fried egg. "Where did you learn to cook this?"

"The cooks at work. We have a cafeteria type thing," he answered with a shrug. "Not what they cook for the workers, but what they cook for themselves. That's where the real food's at. Mostly leftovers, like day old rice, some chopped onions and capsicums and carrot, a bunch of sauces and a crack of chili. Add in a fried egg or two and you got yourself a whole meal."

I nodded as I took another bite. "Do you cook this at home?"

"Sometimes. What about you? What do you cook at home?"

"I don't. If I can avoid it. Just basic stuff." I shrugged. "Growing up, we had whatever was cheap and easy. Meat and veg, basically, because that was all my dad knew how to cook."

"He never remarried?"

I shook my head. "No. He . . . he was never the same after my mother died."

"It must have been hard."

I put my fork on my empty plate. "Yes. Given the public nature of it all. They never should have released the footage. They never asked my dad's permission, and he had to watch his wife die over and over again on every TV channel for weeks. Every time there's a documentary on the dangers of lightning . . ." I sighed. "And it never stops. Still, to this day. Just last year, there was a preview ad for one of those 'history of breaking news stories' shows on TV. Just out of the blue, there she was again, dying in front of him all over again in an ad on the television before he could change the channel."

"Jesus," Tully murmured. "I can't even imagine."

"He doesn't watch much TV now."

"I don't blame him." Tully stacked our plates. "And he doesn't understand why you do what you do?"

"Not at all."

He sighed sadly. "Does he . . . does he know you like men?"

"That I'm gay? Yes. It ranks about fourth on the list of disappointments."

"Only fourth?"

I counted on my fingers. "Number one disappointment is my chosen profession. Number two is that I support Essendon football. Number three is that I don't support Richmond. Number four is I'm gay."

Tully chuckled. "Football, huh?"

"Yes. The one and only thing he will watch on TV is the AFL. He goes to all the games, wears the guernsey and beanie, scarf, the whole thing." I shook my head. "I'm not even that much of a football fan to begin with, to be honest."

"Why Essendon and not Richmond like your dad?"

"When I was about fifteen, he made me go to a game.

Essendon against Richmond. I didn't want to go, made a point of taking a book instead, scowled at everything and everyone, like a typical teen." I rolled my eyes at myself. "Of course we were right up close, by the locker room tunnel. And then I noticed the players."

He grinned at that. "Ohhh. You *noticed* the players."

"Oh yes. It was quite the sexual awakening, seeing them so up close in those tight uniforms, all sweaty and touching each other. One of the players smiled at me as he ran off after the game, and I almost expired on the spot. I've been a loyal Essendon fan ever since."

Tully laughed. "That's poetic."

"My father didn't think so." We stared at each other for a long second, both of us almost smiling. "Your parents know you're . . . bisexual?"

"Sure," he said, waving me off. "Being bisexual made no difference. I mean, out of four kids, they got three straighties and me. Statistically speaking, it was bound to happen. And like I told you already, I'm the baby; the spoiled one. I can do or be whatever and get away with it. Growing up, my eldest brother would get mad because 'oh, the spoiled baby can do whatever he wants' and I'd just laugh and be like 'hell yes, I can, sucks to be you.'" He shrugged with a laugh. "It's the card I was dealt. I use it all the time."

"You have no responsibilities at all?"

"Sure I do. I have bills and a home loan. I have a uni degree I'm still paying off, just like everyone else. I work full-time, and I'm good at what I do. I just choose to do this in my vacation time. You see me here, wearing shorts, no shirt or shoes, and think I live like this. But I don't." He leaned in a whispered like it was a national secret. "I even wear a suit to work."

That made me smile. "I can't imagine it."

Which was a lie because I was imagining it right now . . .

"Well, suit pants, shirt, and tie. It's too hot for a jacket. It's Darwin, after all." He winked. "But some days if I'm just at the office and don't actually have to see people, I can get away with some nice shorts and a company polo shirt. But this?" he gestured to his half naked body. "This is my preferred uniform."

"It suits you."

That cocky smirk was back. "What about you? Please tell me you wear a white lab coat to work."

I snorted. "Why would I wear one of those?"

"Just let me have the fantasy, okay? You would totally rock up in a white lab coat, looking all smart and sexy, studying your data under a microscope."

"I think you have a seriously misconstrued perception about what I actually do for a job."

He laughed. "Let me have the fantasy, Jeremiah. You're not playing the game properly."

I sighed. "Okay, yes. I wear a white lab coat and study data . . . under a micro . . . scope."

Tully laughed, his grin wide. "I'm totally picturing it now. Are you naked under the lab coat?"

"Absolutely not."

"Jeremiah."

"Okay, yes, I'm totally naked. Which would be a violation of almost every occupational health and safety code, but sure. Yes, let's pretend I'm naked."

His eyes did that shining thing when he smiled, which I didn't hate so much anymore. "This is fun. Is there a desk or workstation with computers and shit that you could fuck me on?"

I almost swallowed my tongue.

"Or I could fuck you on it," he added casually. "I don't mind either way. My door swings both ways. Actually, it's not that I don't mind both ways, it's that I prefer both ways. You know, variety is the spice of life. Or something like that."

I was still stuck on his words . . .

that you could fuck me on . . . or I could fuck you on it . . .

His tongue slipped out, wetting his bottom lip before he bit it. "You're picturing it right now, aren't you?"

I shook my head, trying futilely to turn the visuals in my head to mist. Of course that made him laugh. "You totally are. And I'm absolutely regretting not bringing any condoms or lube with me. I didn't think it would be that kind of trip. Unless you brought something with you . . ."

When I still hadn't said anything, he hooked his foot with mine, sliding his up my calf. It startled me out of my thoughts.

"Uh, no. I didn't. I didn't think this trip would be that kind either."

"Do you regret what we've done?" Tully was half-smiling, but his question was serious. He was just hiding it behind his humour.

"Not at all. Do you?"

"Hell no."

I swallowed hard, my mouth dry. "I, uh . . . your door, swinging both ways . . ."

"I just meant that I like to top and bottom."

"Yes, I understood the metaphor."

"Oh."

"I, uh . . ." I needed a sip of water so I could speak.

"I get total top vibes from you," he said, almost cheerfully. "You totally have that sexy in-charge vibe going on. Quiet, super-smart, do-as-I-say vibe. It's hot as fuck."

There he went again, scrambling my thoughts. "Oh."

"Am I right?"

"Well, yes."

"I knew it!"

"But I also like to . . ."

"Take a good dicking?"

I sighed. "Yes. On occasion. If it's with the right person and I can trust them to do it right."

He laughed. "So you gotta be in charge either way."

I scowled at him. "I do not. I'm not—"

"A control freak?"

I gasped, my mouth falling open. "I beg your pardon."

"It's not a bad thing. Like I said, it's hot as fuck. Honestly, I can't wait for you to fuck me. It's gonna be so good."

I blinked a few times, again completely stunned at his boldness. "You're awfully confident to assume that will happen."

He laughed like that was the most ridiculous thing he'd ever heard. Then he stood up, leaning right in close. "Because I know you want to. Hell, it'd almost be worth me driving out of here for two days to find the nearest store that sells supplies." Then he whispered in my ear, his voice low and gruff. "And you want me to fuck you too."

Then he was abruptly gone, taking the plates to the sink, and I sat there too dumbstruck to speak. Hell, I couldn't even form a coherent thought.

Later that night when we climbed into bed, he pulled the sheet up over us, and I expected him to initiate some kind of sex or ask me more personal and embarrassing questions, but he didn't. He sighed into the dark.

"What's your favourite ice cream flavour?"

CHAPTER ELEVEN

TULLY

WE HAD AN EASY MORNING. I MADE US A QUICK breakfast, Jeremiah made the coffee, then we sat around the table going over the data from yesterday and looking to see what was in store for today. The forecast hadn't changed. Storms today and tomorrow, then a shit-ton of rain.

And sure, it could ease up and the forecast could change. The cloud front and low pressure coming in from the Timor Sea could weaken, and maybe we wouldn't have to bunk out.

I didn't want to leave just yet.

I'd thought having some stranger in my space during this trip was going to be annoying, but that couldn't have been further from the truth.

I liked having someone here with me. Not like the time I'd mistakenly asked my brother Ellis to join me. But Jeremiah was like me; he loved the storms, the weather. And he was super smart and he understood the science of it. I was learning a lot and I was already making plans for when I got home to start buying the same gear he had.

It was so freakin' cool.

"So I was thinking," Jeremiah said, not even looking up from his screen.

"Uh oh. Good thinking or bad thinking?"

His eyes met mine then, his brow furrowed. "How is any thinking bad?"

"I'm sorry. What were you thinking?"

"Well, you mentioned the mangroves and the crabs before."

Oh god. I knew where this was going . . . This was bad thinking.

"I think I'd like to see it. During an electrical storm."

"Are you actually insane?"

"No."

"Then why?"

"Mangroves, in particular those with a crustacean colony, emit large quantities of methane and nitrogen, and I'm sure you know what lightning does to areas of ground with high positive charges."

"Yes. That's why I asked you if you were insane." The carcinologists had told me about that. It was why they came here but not normally in the storm season because it was too dangerous. "It's also the wet season. I don't know how accessible they'll be, and I'd need to check the tide chart. And we'd have to camp there overnight. It'd be too far to come back. We'd have to sleep in the Jeep because—"

Jeremiah stood up and closed his laptop. "Then I should start packing."

"—because of the crocodiles." Of course, he acted like he didn't hear me, so I said it again, louder this time. "Because of the crocodiles!"

He started to pack up his equipment crate. "I heard you the first time."

"Then why are you still packing?"

"Because if my time here is being cut short, I need to bring back information. What I have so far is fine, but it's not outstanding, and I need something extraordinary to justify my coming here."

"Okay, cool." I went and threw my bag on the bed, stuffing in a shirt, and did up the zipper. "Have you got your affairs in order?"

"My what?"

"Your affairs. Your papers, your last will and testament." I sprayed myself with insect repellent, and then I did it again. "Because if the lightning don't get ya, the crocs probably will. Or the mozzies." I stopped and looked at him then. "Had a malaria shot? Have you heard of Ross River Fever?"

He scowled at me; his piercing eyes looked like blue fire. "If you're trying to dissuade me, it won't work. It will just make me more determined to go. So if you won't join me, perhaps I can take your vehicle and drive myself."

I tossed the can of insect spray to him. "Oh great. So then I'd have to walk outta here to get you some help. Stellar idea, genius. Just out of curiosity, where would you like your body shipped to? If they find your body, that is. Usually a croc will just take ya into deeper waters and pummel you a bit, leave you stuffed under a log or something, till you're nice and tender. Bodies are rarely recovered. They just find finger marks dug into the riverbank and they stop looking. Call off the search parties right then and there."

He was staring at me now. "Are you finished?"

"Not even close." I sniffed. "Now, mangroves in particular have high concentrations of lightning strikes—"

He sighed loud enough to stop me. "Which is why I'm going. So, you can either come with me or I can go in alone."

I glared at him.

He glared right back at me.

And for the longest moment, neither one of us blinked. I caved first, snarling at him for good measure. "Did you major in stubbornness at university?"

"I have a doctorate."

"In stubbornness."

"Actually—"

"In *stubborn*ness."

Then he sighed and I felt like we were on a seesaw, where neither one of us would ever get the advantage.

He glowered. I huffed.

He mumbled under his breath while he packed up his own shit, I lowered the walls and closed the place up. We would likely be back, but it wasn't guaranteed, so I treated it like we were leaving for good.

We drove the Jeep out in silence.

"ARE YOU DRIVING RECKLESSLY ON PURPOSE?" he asked. The track was bad, and he was holding onto the oh-shit bar, giving me the stink eye every chance he got.

"Yes, I designed this track to have more craters than the moon, and I'm choosing to hit every single hole in hopes that I break the suspension so we get stranded out here because, honestly, getting taken by a croc and enduring one of the most painful deaths ever is preferable to whatever your fuckin' problem is."

He glowered at me even harder as we bounced through another bad part of the track. "And you think I'm stubborn."

"No, I think you're stupid. Incredibly intelligent, and really fuckin' stupid."

Aaaaand that earned me some more silence.

And then I felt bad.

But this *was* stupid. And he knew the risks and he still wanted to go. And I was stupid enough to be going with him.

Did that make me stupider?

Goddammit.

After a long stretch of silence and a lot of bumpy kilo-metres under the tyres, I knew I had to break the silence. "I'll need you to navigate," I said. "Can you see if you can get any signal for a map on your iPad?"

"Do you not know where we're going?"

"Not really. I've been out here once in the dry season. It looks a little different now."

He baulked then, schooling his reaction, quickly took out his iPad, and tapped the screen a few times. "Nothing."

"Shit."

"I have the paper map," he said, pulling it out of his bag. "I don't know how detailed it will be for these parts."

Not very, I thought. But I didn't say that.

He unfolded it and refolded it so he could see roughly where we were. "Our camp was here," he said, bouncing in his seat but not taking his eyes or finger off the map. "We took the north road out, turned off to go due east to the South Alligator River, about ten k's along . . ." He checked the scale of the map, then checked his watch. "Considering our distance over time, we should be approximately here." He held his finger to a certain point on the map. "Meaning we have about another five to eight kilometres to go."

It irked me that he used intelligence, reasoning, and common sense. "Thank you."

The forest around us had changed. No longer paperbarks and plum trees, it was now palms and mangroves, and the track was becoming more sandy. "I don't know how much further we'll be able to go by car," I said. "I won't risk getting us bogged in sand before high tide comes in. We'll have to park, then walk in for a bit."

He looked at me, then out the windscreen at the swampiness of our surroundings. And a look of 'shit, what have I done?' flashed in his eyes before he schooled that away too. He gave a nod. "Okay."

The track got sandier and sandier, and at the next part of the track with anything close to a turning area, I pulled us up to a slow stop. "Okay, this'll have to do us." Doing a quick three-point turn, I turned the Jeep around so we were facing the way we'd come.

"What are you doing?"

I pointed ahead to our escape route. "In case we need to leave in a hurry."

I didn't miss the way he swallowed, but with nothing else said, he got out of the Jeep and began arranging his gear.

"Take only what you can carry," I said, takin' his map and giving it a once over. He'd done a pretty good job of giving us an estimated location. These tracks off the main road weren't marked on any map, so I had to give credit where it was due. "You were pretty good with the map," I said, aiming for nonchalant. I wasn't goin' for friendly, but at least we were talking again. I turned the map over and scribbled out a quick note to leave in the Jeep, should someone come across it or if we didn't come back. At least the cops'd be able to tell the coroner our cause of death was stupidity.

Gone into mangroves on foot. Two men sat phone and water. One day at most.

I shoved it on the dash, then remembered to add the date at the bottom.

Realising Jeremiah hadn't replied, I looked over to see what he was doing . . . to find him emptying out my bag and adding his gear to it.

"What the hell do you think you're doing?"

He looked up, confused. "I'm taking as much as I can carry."

"That's my bag."

"Yes. I'm aware."

I got out and walked around to his side, grabbing his hand on my bag. "Don't touch my stuff."

His steely blue eyes met mine. "I was simply being efficient."

We were standing close, eye to eye. Well, he was a few inches taller than me, but still. My grip on his hand tightened. "You shoulda asked."

His nostrils flared and his jaw clenched. I would've found that hot if he didn't piss me off so much. Hell, maybe he was hot *because* he pissed me off so much. He yanked his hand away. "Forget it. I'll carry it in the crate."

He leaned over to pull the crate closer, but I finished shoving his gear into my bag. "All you hadta do was ask," I said as I shoved in the spinning thing from the top of his auto-station. He'd dumped the first aid kit out of my bag so I picked it up. "And where the hell are ya goin' without this?"

"I was going to put it on top."

He absolutely was not.

I picked up the can of spray paint he'd ditched and glared at him.

Christ almighty.

He wiped the sweat from his brow and I noticed then just how much he was sweating. It was hot, and it was muggy as hell. I kept forgetting how he wasn't used to the tropics . . . "Here, drink some water," I said, handin' him a bottle. "Sip it. No gulping."

He gave me another glare for good measure, but he did drink some water.

When he was done packin' up his bags, he slung his backpack on, then reached for my bag and slung the long strap over his head and one shoulder.

"What are you doing?" I asked.

"Taking as much as I can carry."

I took my bag off him, lifting the strap over his head. "I can carry this."

He looked at me as if he really wanted to say something, but he shut his mouth and looked away. "Fine. Whatever. Thanks, I guess. Sorry for being so stupid."

I put the bag over my head and one shoulder and let out a groan and handed him the tripod to carry. "Look, I'm sorry for the stupid comment. I shouldn't have said that. You're not stupid. You're the smartest person I know."

He looked away, petulantly, and I watched as a bead of sweat ran down from his temple, along his jaw and down the column of his neck.

I shouldn't want to lick that . . .

I shook my head, getting back on track. "So, I'm sorry. I apologise. You're not stupid."

He pouted. "Fine. Thank you."

God, I wanted to strangle him. I also wanted to kiss him and do obscene things to his body, but mostly I wanted to strangle him. "But what you're *doing* is stupid. Just so we're clear."

He growled. Literally fucking growled at me.

My whole body reacted and I grunted, having to readjust myself. "Damn."

He squinted at me. "If we're discussing the measuring parameters of stupid."

"That was hot as fuck. Can you growl at me again?"

He rolled his eyes and stomped off, following the track.

"Jeremiah?" I called out.

He spun around. "What?"

Grinning, I pointed with my thumb into the scrub. "We gotta go this way."

I set off, not looking to see if he followed or not. The ground was wet sand and we had to climb over mangrove roots and branches. Our boots were sinking a little, nothing too bad yet, but it was definitely getting wetter the further we went.

I could hear Jeremiah behind me, his feet and the occasional grunt as he scaled a mangrove root. I was sweating now, so he had to be feelin' it. Taking the can of paint, I sprayed a pink stripe across a tree every ten metres or so.

"Is that your version of a Hansel and Gretel breadcrumb?"

"That's exactly what it is. So we can find our way outta here." I looked back. "Wanna stop for a bit?"

He glanced skyward. "No, not yet. Those clouds are coming in."

Awesome.

Can't wait.

"Don't look so thrilled," he said, brushing past me to take the lead.

"Okay, you go first," I said sarcastically. "Your turn to be on the lookout for all the things that can kill us."

"You're not funny."

I wasn't bein' funny, but okay. "Yep, I'm hilarious."

"These roots would make it impossible for crocs to navigate anyway," he said, like I was lying to him about it.

"Like this? Correct. But I'm tellin' ya, come high tide, we are back at the Jeep. Understood?"

He shot me a glance over his shoulder. I'm pretty sure he rolled his eyes.

We walked, climbed, and jumped over branches for a good while in silence. Our shoes were now sinking with each step, and all I could think about was our ability to get out of here once the water started coming in. Thankfully not too much further we came to a bit of a clearing in the mangroves.

I had my shirt off, dripping sweat. Jeremiah hung his backpack on a tree root, and liftin' his shirt up, he wiped his face with it. "Christ, how do people live here?" he griped.

"You get used to it. Drink more water."

He didn't need telling twice. He sipped his bottle and wiped his face again.

"Take your shirt off," I said.

"I think I'm better off with it on."

"I think the view is better with it off."

He glared.

I smiled.

"I'm immune to the smile now."

I let my head fall back. "Aww. It's my only party trick."

He ignored me, and extending the tripod legs, he sunk it into the sand. "Help me get this set up."

He went about setting all his contraptions up, checkin' to see what readings he could get while I kept checking the water at our feet.

Dark storm clouds rumbled above us, expanding and rolling like living entities. Intra-cloud lightning sparked inside them and the wind picked up.

"Here, hold this," he said, handing me the display screen. He positioned the small radar at the top of the auto-station, and while it rotated, the screen beeped. "This is gonna be a good one," he said, excited.

For crying out loud.

"You know, I know this place is called Kakadu, but there's probably more Kaka-don'ts than there are Kaka-do's."

Jeremiah sighed, deflated, and he deadpanned a stare at me. "How long have you been waiting to use that joke?"

I laughed. "A while."

He rolled his eyes.

"But yeah, about the Kaka-don'ts," I continued, "I'd probably think standing in the middle of the mangroves with an electrical storm brewin' while holding a radar device up to the sky—*while standing in two inches of sandy water*—is high on that list."

"You knew the risks," he mumbled.

"What can I say," I said flatly. "I didn't want you to die alone."

"I don't plan on dying here today."

"Pretty sure no one plans to get struck by lightning."

His eyes cut to mine.

"Except for you," I added.

He went back to ignoring me, reading his machines, all while the winds picked up and the storm darkened.

"Why do I have a bad feeling about this?" I asked.

"Because you're a pessimist."

I gasped. "I am not."

Jeremiah raised one eyebrow. "You need to trust the science."

"I do trust science. But lightning is a great unknown. Unpredictable, dangerous. You can't harness it or control it. You can study it your whole damn life and still won't know all there is to know because you can't put it in a lab. You can try to recreate it, but it won't be the same."

He was staring at me. "So should I stop? Should I just never try because you think it's impossible?"

"No, I—"

"I could almost guarantee you that every scientist who did something great was told they were foolish for trying. Do you think the scientists who try to create cold fusion are wasting their time? They're so close to breakthroughs that could solve the world energy crisis, yet people dismiss it because they think it's impossible."

"No, that's not—"

His eyes met mine, cold and blue. "I don't know why I thought you were different." He snatched the RF antenna out of his bag, ignoring me.

I wasn't expectin' his bite to hurt so much. "Jeremiah," I murmured.

A clap of thunder cracked right above us, makin' me duck on instinct. Of course, Jeremiah didn't even flinch, with his back to me, his shirt blowing in the wind.

Jesus Christ.

I opened my mouth to tell him I was sorry just as the clouds opened up instead. Rain, fat drops, truckloads of them, heavy and drenching. It was falling so hard I could barely see Jeremiah just a few metres away.

"Well, that's fuckin' great," I yelled over the rain.

But then it got even greater.

Thunder and sheet lightning, the clouds so low and close it felt as if I could touch them. More intra-cloud lightning lit up around us like a strobe party and I had an eerie realisation.

We could *actually* die out here.

For real. No jokes, no snarky comebacks. For actual real.

"Jeremiah," I yelled again.

He turned to look at me then.

That fucker was grinning. "This is awesome!"

He trudged back to the screen like he was having the best experience of his life.

For fuck's sake. I was beginning to think he was legitimately insane.

He zipped up his backpack in the pouring rain, and taking the screen from me, he handed me the backpack. "Hold this!"

Thunder boomed again, so loud and so close that it shook us both. Cracking and rumbling, non-stop now, the clouds so dark that flashes of lightning were the only way I could see.

"This is crazy," I yelled.

Thunder ripped so loud it hurt my ears, and lightning struck about a hundred metres away. I must have jumped a metre in the air, my heart was hammerin' to the point of pain. That was far, far too close.

"Jeremiah!"

He held up two fingers. "Two more minutes!"

"Now!"

He shook his head.

I unzipped my bag and shoved the screen in it, then began pulling pieces off the station. We were done here. This was stupid and crazy, and he was in-fucking-sane if he thought we were staying in this. The anemometer was spinning so fast—the wind was in a frenzy, blowin' the rain in all directions, but I unhooked it anyway. We were leaving, whether he liked it or not.

The thunder was constant and the lightning all too frequent, and far too fuckin' close.

And if that wasn't bad enough, it was then I noticed his shoes. They were completely underwater. I looked at mine. The water was up to my ankles.

"Jeremiah, now!"

He turned then, his hair stuck to his forehead, water pouring from his chin, and I don't know what he saw on my face but it made him pause. I pointed to his feet. "We have to go!"

He was clearly surprised to see his feet underwater. He nodded quickly, and we packed up, shoving everything into any bag. It didn't matter. He folded up the tripod and began for the return trip and stopped. "Which way?"

It was hard to tell now that everything looked different. Our footprints were all underwater and washed away, but there was a pink stripe on a tree to our left. "This way."

Going back was harder and slower. The rain was whipping us, and we were trudging through almost shin-deep water and waterlogged sand. We had to climb and hurdle branches, and I held my hand out for Jeremiah to hold as he swung his legs over one in particular.

Then something splashed in the water behind us.

I pulled Jeremiah in front of me. "Move," I yelled. "Go, go!"

Like the storm was keeping tempo with us, thunder rumbled and roared and lightning put on a light show around us. And we hightailed it as fast as we could. My heart was in my throat the whole freaking way. I had scratches up my legs and hands, but I didn't care.

High tide was comin' in way too fast with the storm.

We passed more trees with the paint spray, and the further we went, the more the water level dropped and the sand was firmer underfoot until Jeremiah stopped. He put his hand on a tree root, bent over, trying to catch his breath.

"What did you stop for? Keep going."

He pointed his chin further along where, through the mangroves, I could see the Jeep.

Oh, thank god.

I sighed, taking in gulping breaths of air.

The rain had eased up a bit, the storm clouds had mostly passed over us, leaving behind the setting sun, humidity, and the sounds of birds and cicadas.

"We can stop when we're in the Jeep," I said, urging him to push on. "High tide's coming in faster than us."

With a nod, he collected himself, scaled the tree root, and walked the final distance to the embankment and up to the Jeep. He dumped his backpack, his hands on his hips, panting. "That was fun."

Fun. Did he just say . . .

"Fun?" I pointed to the way we'd come. "We almost died. Several times."

He smirked. "I got some good readings."

I threw my hands up. "Well, that makes dying all worth it then, doesn't it?"

He laughed, walked over to me, took hold of my face in

his dirty hands, and kissed me. A big wet smacker on the lips. "Thank you."

He was giving me whiplash.

"What for?"

"For bringing me here. For doing this. For marking the trees. That was a really great idea."

"The crab people told me they do that," I mumbled. "They had cans of spray paint. I asked them what it was for."

He grinned and moved some hair from my forehead with his finger. So gently, sweetly. "And you put yourself between me and whatever that thing was that splashed in the water. I mean, it was probably just a fish or something, but still . . . It was sweet. Thank you."

"It probably wasn't a fish, just so you know. It was probably a croc or maybe a northern river shark, given the water wasn't very deep. But it's the smaller ones you gotta be careful of. The small crocs are the dangerous ones. They're fast and—"

He cupped my face and pulled me in for another kiss. It was deeper this time, open mouths and a little tongue, and a very effective way to shut me up, apparently. It also made all my anger melt away, and my desire to wring his neck was more desire to keep kissing him.

When he pulled back, he was smiling. "We should probably try and get cleaned up."

"Probably."

We were drenched, from our dripping hair to our sodden boots half-filled with sand, but by the time we managed to dry off and clean up a bit, it was getting on dusk and the water was right up to the embankment and I had the eerie feeling of being watched.

So, barefoot and with a decent spray of insect repellent, we got into the Jeep. We ate baked beans straight from the can, then put the front seats back as far as they'd go, which wasn't far, and looked out the windscreen as the clouds were replaced by a brilliant cover of stars.

"It's so easy to see why the First Nations people believe their gods come from the stars," Jeremiah said quietly. "It's so beautiful."

I turned to look at him, his face silver in the moonlight. Speaking of beautiful . . .

Then, ruining the serenity of that moment, he sat up in his seat. "I need to pee." He went to open the door and I grabbed his arm.

"No!" I barked. Then I turned on the headlights to show him why. A dozen sets of eyes glinted back at us, and five or so crocs slithered off the road as the light hit them.

He shrank back in his seat, bringing his arms in and legs up. He was now deathly pale.

"Still need to pee?"

He shook his head. "No."

I laughed and, reaching into the back, found him an empty water bottle. "If you get desperate, pee into that."

He shot me a wild look. "Ew."

Chuckling, I turned the headlights off and lay back down in my seat. It was dark and quiet, but after a few minutes, I heard the rustle of clothes and then the sound of him pissing into the bottle. I laughed.

"I hate you," he mumbled.

I snorted. "No you don't."

When he was done, he tossed it out the window. "I'll pick it up tomorrow. Then we shall never talk about it again."

I smiled into the dark, and after a while, I reached for his arm and pulled his hand into mine. I threaded our fingers and closed my eyes.

"Jeremiah," I mumbled sleepily.

"Yes?"

"What's your favourite colour?"

CHAPTER TWELVE

JEREMIAH

I BARELY SLEPT, KNOWING THERE WERE CROCODILES outside the Jeep. I kept waiting to hear a thunk or scraping noises. Even though I knew, rationally, it wasn't likely that a crocodile would try to climb or attack a vehicle, it didn't stop my imagination from running wild.

Mangroves were noisy too. Birds and cicadas sang to us all night. And I totally did not lie there watching Tully as he slept, at how his eyelashes cast shadows on his cheeks, at the cupid's bow of his lips, at the three-day growth, the wisps of his wild and wavy hair. I longed to run my fingers through it, but of course I didn't.

He'd perhaps saved my life today.

In all likelihood, I'd have been caught by the rapidly rising tide—I hadn't realised just how fast it would come in. And the paint marks on the tree. I wouldn't have done that, and after being turned around and blinded by the storm, I'd have got lost for sure. Lost in a rapidly rising high tide in crocodile infested mangroves. And then, with the loud splash behind us in the water, he'd put himself in harm's way instead of me . . .

Not to mention the lightning.

The storm had been low and powerful. High energy, low barometric pressure, strong winds, and a lot of electrical activity, and I couldn't wait for sunrise to get back and run the data.

Even though it meant another day down meant one less day here. One less day with Tully.

I liked him.

He infuriated me, but he challenged me. I was mad that he'd not understood my reason for wanting to come to the mangroves, but I could see now that his concern was for our safety.

And he'd been right, of course.

But so had I.

I needed to prove to my colleagues in Melbourne that I was serious and not just the weirdo they all thought I was. I needed to bring back data they had neither the aptitude nor the balls to get.

And maybe I did that today.

I hoped so, anyway.

Daylight crept over the horizon, the skies a pastel palette of pinks and oranges. I was relieved to see the road was clear of crocodiles, and from my seat, it looked as if the water had receded, taking the crocodiles with it.

I still wasn't getting out of the Jeep until Tully gave me the all-clear. After all, it was never the crocs you could see that you should be worried about. It was always the ones you couldn't see . . .

I made a point of sitting up with a loud yawn and stretch, then righting my seat with a clunk, and it worked. Tully cracked one eye open, scrubbed his faced with his hands, then sat up. "Did we survive?"

"Yes. Thanks to you. Are all the crocodiles gone?"

He looked out the front windshield and down his side of the Jeep. "Looks like it. The water's low."

"Am I right to get out?"

He nodded, and when I'd opened my door an inch, he said, "Unless there's one under the Jeep."

I might have screamed and pulled the door shut, bringing my legs up onto my seat. I don't know why.

He laughed, and I shoved his arm. "That's not funny."

"Kinda was," he said, getting out of the Jeep without a care in the world. He stood up, stretched his hands above his head, and yawned.

I hated that he was so attractive the second he woke up.

And cheerful.

Jerk.

I got out with a huff, and seeing Tully peeing into the mangroves on his side of the Jeep, I did the same on my side. Then I remembered the bottle I'd thrown out the window during the night and went to find it . . .

"Oh my god," I said, trudging a few metres into the mangroves. The sand was dry, thankfully, and it was easy to walk on, given I was barefoot. The water bottle that I'd relieved myself in last night was now about five metres from the track, completely empty and crumpled flat with several large puncture marks.

I picked it up, horrified, and got my arse back to the Jeep as fast as I could. I held it up to show Tully. "Look at this."

His eyes widened as he realised what he was looking at. "Holy shit. Is that the bottle you pissed in?"

"It has to be," I said, looking around. There was no other litter anywhere, and it was the same brand. "Look at the teeth marks." I could stick my index finger through the holes.

Tully took the bottle, like it was the best thing he'd ever seen. "He drank your electrolytes . . ." Then he laughed. "Oh my god, it's Gatorade! Get it? Gator-ade. Except it's Croc-ade."

I sighed. "That's not funny."

He clearly thought it was hilarious. "I'm keeping this," he said.

"I urinated in it!"

He held it out and shook it. "There's no piss in it now. The croc drank it all."

I rolled my eyes, obviously not going to win here at all, and got in the Jeep. "Can we please go now?"

He took the roof off the Jeep so everything could dry out a little and we drove for a while, the track now noticeably different. The craters and holes were filled with water and it was slower going, and it wasn't until we got back on the larger track—I still wouldn't call it a road—that I could stop holding onto the grab bar long enough to rummage through our gear for some fruit.

I handed him an apple, which he took with a grin. "Thanks."

I ate half mine in just a few bites, not realising how hungry I was. "I'm really looking forward to a shower. I feel gross."

"You look just fine to me," he said, his hair tousled in the breeze, his carefree smile and kind eyes making my heart stutter. He ate the rest of his apple before tossing the core out of the Jeep. "What?" he asked at my questioning stare. "It'll feed the birds or plant a tree."

So I finished my apple and did the same, earning me a grin from Tully.

"You know," he said over the wind and the engine. "We should probably shower together. Conserve the water consumption."

"Given it's the wet season and it dumps a truckload of water every afternoon, I doubt the shower tank will run out of water."

He laughed. "Can't be too careful."

BACK AT THE CAMP, we lifted the walls of the bunker to let some air in, then we unloaded the Jeep. Tully checked for any snakes or frogs, and I made us some coffee and set my gear up.

We made a good team.

Which was a first for me, because I rarely worked well with anyone else. Well, I liked it just fine. Usually it was the other person who didn't like working with me. I was too *pedantic* or a *control freak*. Which, as I'd told my boss when he'd requested a meeting with me to discuss this problem, was honestly them admitting their standards weren't high enough.

I wasn't looking forward to going back . . .

"What's up?" Tully asked. He sipped his coffee. "You just sighed twice in thirty seconds."

I made a third just for good measure. "Nothing. Just . . . I'm not looking forward to returning to my office in Melbourne."

He nodded to my gear on the table. "But you have all this new data."

"And it's good." I put my cup down. "Well, I'm hoping what we collected yesterday is great. I need . . ."

"You need to justify the expense of you coming here," he finished for me.

"Yes. But I also need to prove that I'm capable and that I do take the science of this very seriously. It's not just about me being fascinated by lightning because . . . because of what happened." I breathed in deep and let it out slowly. "I need to prove that I'm better than them. I *am* better than them. Just because I'm not in their little clique, and because I don't sit at the cool kid's table. I'm sick of that bullshit. I want to take this data back to them and say, 'hey, look at what you can actually do if you took your head out of your arse.'"

Tully laughed, his eyes wide in surprise. "I'd like to see that."

"I am serious about this. I want to further the field and understand what I can, in hopes of reducing the likelihood of strike fatalities. Of course, that's a priority. But there's more to it than that."

"It's personal to you," he said quietly. He reached over

and took my hand. "They'll never understand that. They'll never understand you. So don't let them. And that cool club cliquey shit is high school all over again. Fuck that shit. And fuck them."

I snorted. "True." I studied his hand over mine, and when he went to pull it away, I quickly threaded our fingers. "Thank you."

He gave me a shy smile, then he took my hand and examined my knuckles, then my fingernails. He stood up and pulled me to my feet. "You need a shower. And I need to inspect you do a thorough job."

I would have objected, but he stripped me naked and pushed me into the shower, sliding himself up against me, using his talented hands to scrub me clean, and his mouth . . . my god, the way he used his mouth . . .

I returned the favour, eagerly going to my knees for him like he had for me.

And afterwards, he took a nap on the bed while I downloaded all the data from the day before. Though I kept looking over at Tully. He looked so peaceful, so comfortable, I wanted nothing more than to forget work for a moment and join him.

So I did.

I lay down beside him and he immediately rolled over and threw his arm and leg over me. I smiled into his chest. He pressed a soft kiss to my forehead. I closed my eyes, smiling, probably happier in that moment than I'd ever been.

And we slept.

"Shit," Tully said. "Wake up, wake up."

I sat up, dazed and confused. I'd been so sound asleep, it took me a second to even remember where I was.

Then I noticed the radar beeping and the wind outside. Shit.

Storm, incoming.

"Help me get the side down," he said, running to the far end of the shed. "It's coming in from the east. It's gonna be a good one."

I raced to my end of the shed and we got the wall down, the wind fighting us the whole way. Once it was locked down, we lowered the other side halfway, then ducked under it to take a look at the sky.

Dark, foreboding, and as Tully said, coming in from the wrong direction. The trees were whipped around in a fury, and thunder began to roll.

He clapped my back. "Let's get your gear set up."

I followed him, both of us racing back inside. He took the auto-station, and without me asking him to, he raced it to the far end of the clearing to set it up. I gave him a thumbs up when I got the first readings, and he raced back, quickly checking the camera screens as soon as he came in, while I opened the radars.

"How does it look?" he asked.

"It's a wide front," I replied. "About ten kilometres from our location but heading straight toward us. It's moving pretty fast." I pointed to the band of clouds with multiple white dots. "High electrical activity and hail."

"Excellent."

"I know—"

It was only when I looked at his face that I could tell he was being sarcastic.

"Yeah okay," I mumbled.

He walked back toward the door. "Help me throw the tarp over the Jeep."

It was a heavy sheet of army green canvas, and it took both of us to secure it with the wind. By the time we got it done, the rain had started.

It was thin and needle-like in the wind, and I was glad when Tully pulled me inside and shut the door behind us. "Whoo," he said on a breath. "It's gonna be a good'n."

He went to check the radar and the readouts, excited as I was, and it thrilled me that he loved this part as much as me.

The build-up, the anticipation before the storm hit. The way the air grew thick and dense, ripening the atmosphere for lightning.

Thunder rolled and a crack boomed not far from us. Maybe five kilometres away, and my excitement grew even more.

"I can't believe we slept that long," Tully said.

Neither could I. We'd napped for hours. "I didn't wake once," I admitted. "As soon as you put your arm over me, it was lights out for me."

He tried to rein in his smile. "I didn't expect you to join me."

"I barely slept at all last night. Kept waiting for a crocodile to open the door or climb onto the Jeep and fall through the canopy top."

He laughed, just as a boom of thunder shook the shed and lightning lit up the darkened sky outside. The radar warning started to beep on my laptop, and we flew into action.

"Jesus, it looks wild out there," Tully said, his eyes glued to the camera screen. "I'm gonna put the other wall down to the ground."

I nodded. "Good idea."

The footage outside showed the trees being whipped in all directions, the cloud cover was low and heavy, swelling and rolling. Lightning sent its spidery fingers through the clouds, cracking and hissing, sending forks to the ground in the forest around us. Rain pummelled the bunker, the wind was roaring, rattling the shed, and I couldn't hear anything over the furore of it all.

I saw the automatic station get ripped from the ground, and a second later, the wind data cut.

Dammit.

Tully grabbed my arm and he had to yell so I could hear him. "Leave it. It's too dangerous. There are trees down out there."

I looked at the footage screen and saw a small branch shoot across the clearing.

I nodded, because even I knew that it was too dangerous to go out in.

And then the water canister flew across the clearing.

Jesus.

It was deafening, but somehow the bunker remained unscathed. Oh, it rattled and protested, but it held . . .

Then a familiar and dreadful taste filled my mouth. It was cloying and strong. It was going to be close.

Shit.

"Lightning!" I yelled.

Tully spun to face me, confused, just as thunder boomed so close, so loud, it almost knocked us off our feet. And with a flash of bright light outside, a massive crack ripped through the bunker. Deafening.

Frightening.

The power board exploded, sparks flying.

Tully lunged for me, grabbing me, pulling me close and wrapping his arms around me, ducking my head to his chest. My ears popped, and for one moment, all I could hear was his heart, his pulse. Or maybe it was mine. Our panting breaths, one arm around my back, the other holding my head.

He was protecting me.

After a few heart-thumping minutes, the sound of the rain and wind died off, whether the storm had lessened any or if it was just my hearing, I couldn't be sure.

But he held me until our chests stopped heaving. When he slowly pulled me back, I saw the look of fear on his face. He was a shade paler, his eyes wide. There was the pungent smell of smoke, but thankfully no fire. The power board was still smouldering.

"Did we just get struck by lightning?"

I swallowed thickly, the acrid copper taste lingering in my mouth. "The bunker, yes." The lightning rods on the roof worked.

When he let go of me, I noticed his hands were shaking. I quickly grabbed one hand and held it, squeezing. "Are you okay?"

He ran his other hand through his hair, looked around the room, bewildered. He went over to the power board and pulled it from the power socket. "Uh, yeah. I think so."

I needed a drink. My tongue felt putrid. I guzzled half a bottle. It didn't make it much better.

"You knew we were about to get hit," Tully said, stating the obvious.

I shot him a look. "Yes. I can still taste it."

He put his hand on my back. "Do you feel okay?"

"I'm fine. Physically. And you?"

He half shrugged, then grabbed my wrist and looked at my watch. "Heart rate's up."

"I bet yours is too."

I nodded toward my gear on the table—no lights were flashing anymore. "We've lost power."

"Video's still recording," he said, going over for a closer look. "The one that you run separately. Looks like the worst of the storm has passed us."

It was still raining, and the wind was still toying with the trees and there was debris, branches and leaves, strewn across the clearing, but it was nowhere near as strong.

"We should check your Jeep," I said, given it was our transport out.

"And your auto-station," he said. "It's probably wrapped around a tree." Then he pointed to the ceiling. "I'll need to check your booster. Maybe it got blown over."

"Or fried."

He grimaced, then let out a long sigh. "I can't believe we got hit by lightning. That shit is scary as fuck."

"Thank god whoever built this put lightning rods on the roof. Or you and I would both be dead, more than likely."

His eyes met mine, solemn and grim with the confirmation of just how close we came, and he nodded.

"Okay, help me get the walls up." He stopped before he touched the crank handle and pulled his arm back. "Uh, is this safe to touch?"

"Yes. Lightning rods have metal tracks to the ground that divert the power. Once it earths, it's fine."

He still wasn't too keen to put his hand on it, so I took the water bottle and threw a spray of water against it. Nothing sizzled or sparked. "Phew," he said, gingerly touching the handle with the back of his hand. "Okay, it's fine."

Once we got the walls up, the rain had eased to a gentle drizzle and the wind had died down too. We stepped outside and took stock of the damage.

The Jeep had a branch on it, but thankfully the windscreen and windows were intact. It was pretty much soaked, but otherwise unscathed. The water canister was at the tree line on the side of the clearing. Tully set off to collect it, and I headed to the far end to look for my automatic weather station.

It wasn't in the clearing, so I headed to the tree line at the top end. I picked up some smaller branches that were strewn and tossed them into the trees so they wouldn't become a missile in the next storm.

Then I trekked into the trees a little, and sure enough, noticed the tripod about twenty metres in. It was on its head, broken, and half wrapped around a tree. The screen was smashed, the anemometer arms and the sensors were broken.

Goddammit.

I inspected it, not hopeful it could be repaired. But the

equipment box looked mostly undamaged. Hopefully I could salvage some data . . .

I headed back to the shed, only to find Tully climbing up onto the roof.

Because he hadn't almost died enough times in the last twenty-four hours.

"Please be careful," I yelled.

He waved and carefully trod across the ridgeline, where he stopped at what I could now see was the booster, which he'd MacGyvered for me on our first day. He picked it up—clearly it was no longer secured—and I could see why we'd lost our signal.

It was a lump of black melted goo.

"Ah," he said, tossing it onto the grass below. "Don't touch it. It's still kinda hot."

I went to inspect it and, yeah, it was almost unrecognisable.

Tully climbed down, dusting his hands off as he came to stand beside me. "RIP that thing," he said. "Was that what the lightning hit? Or did it just get fried for being so close to the rod?"

I used the broken tripod to turn the melted booster over on the grass. "Hard to tell. But just fried from being so close, I'd think. If it was a direct hit, it'd be blown to smithereens."

He took the tripod, and when he held it up, it bent in the middle. "Jeez, this is shot too."

I nodded, unable to hide my disappointment. "Yeah."

He looked at me, studying my face for a few seconds. "You know what I think? I think this gear is replaceable." He poked me in the chest. "You, are not."

I half shrugged. I knew what he said was true, but damn . . .

"I know," I whispered. "It's just . . . it's not replaceable. Not for me anyway."

I unfastened the data box and threw the broken tripod by the door, with all the other scrap material, and went inside. I closed my laptop—there was no point in staring at a black screen. And I watched Tully on the camera screen. He was standing right where I'd left him outside. He ran his hand through his hair and went toward the door. He disappeared off the screen as he walked inside.

I threw myself on the bed with a sigh and slung my arm over my eyes.

A few moments later, Tully knelt over me and peeled my arm away. "Hey," he said. "Talk to me."

I was being petulant. I knew I was. But still . . . I couldn't help the way I felt.

"My gear isn't replaceable because I have no money, and now that I have no gear, I can't do anything. I'm leaving in two days and now I have to go back without my instruments, without any data," I gestured to the table, "because it's probably all fried, and it just feels like a failure. The way they all expected me to fail. As if I'm proving those arseholes right. And all I wanted was to go back and prove to them I was worthy. Now I don't want to go back at all."

Well, that came out a lot easier than I expected. I surprised myself by how easy it was to tell him this. How easy it was to talk to him.

I tried to pull my arm free so I could cover my face, cover my shame, but he tightened his grip and pinned me to the bed. His eyes bored into mine. "Hey. You listen to me. You're not a failure. You lived through two electrical storms in two days. Closer to lightning than we had any right to be. I bet those pen-pushin' nerds you work with ain't ever been that close to any storm in their miserable lives. You got good data. Data you can analyse for months. Data that will give you new information, new findings. And then those arseholes will know just how good you are." He straddled me, sitting his full weight on me, and he let go of my arms. "Now about your gear, don't worry about that. I can get you new stuff."

"You don't have to do—"

"Yeah, I do. Because I'm pretty sure the way I MacGyvered your booster thing is what blew it out." He shrugged. "So it's technically my fault."

"No you didn't. You used no metal. Just wood and zip ties."

He leaned down and kissed me. "Shh. It was my fault."

"Tully—"

He pinned my hands above my head this time. "I said shh," he said with a sultry smile. "All your equipment is off, it's raining outside. There is nothing for me to do . . . except you."

I would have objected—I fully intended to object—but he ground down on me, rubbing himself, and my hips rolled involuntarily. Smirking, he put his knees between my legs and drove my legs apart.

I gasped, and my watch started beeping like crazy . . .

He laughed and I rolled my eyes, but then he kissed me, deep and filthy, until nothing else existed. No money problems, no work problems, no almost-dying twice in twenty-four hours, no leaving this place, and not my stupid watch that only stopped beeping when Tully pulled it off my wrist.

Nothing but him and the obscenely good things he did to my body.

CHAPTER THIRTEEN
TULLY

Somethin' was different with Jeremiah after that last storm. I understood about his gear and not havin' the money to replace it. And I understood that he needed to prove to his jerk colleagues back in Melbourne that he was more than a guy just obsessed with lightning.

He was a scientist. He was intelligent, and he had guts. He was determined and driven.

All he wanted was to be taken seriously and to be credited with his work.

And maybe he was extra bummed about not being able to read any of his data because his booster was a melted pile of metal and plastic. Or maybe he lost the data. We wouldn't know until he could get a look at it. And that was deflating.

But it wasn't just that.

That last storm had shaken him.

"You sure you're okay?" I asked.

We were sitting cross-legged on the bed with bowls of rice in our laps. He'd barely touched his dinner. Even after the mind-blowin' afternoon we'd spent in bed, his mood hung heavy around him like the clouds outside.

"Yeah," he answered, more of a hum than a word.

"We have to leave tomorrow," I said, not for the first time. I pointed to the sound of rain on the roof. "This is the real beginning of the rainy season. They've predicted two days of heavy falls and that means all roads in and out will be underwater. Unless you wanna get choppered out, or if you wanna stay here for three or four months . . ."

His eyes cut to mine, and I realised I'd said the magic words.

He didn't just not want to go back to Melbourne and back to work. He didn't want to go back at all.

"I'd like to stay here," he said quietly. "I know it's not possible or feasible, at all. We'd be out of food in a few days, and I don't fancy eating crocodile."

"It's not so much the eatin' crocs that's questionable," I said, trying to lighten the mood. "It's the catchin' of the croc that's problematic."

He shrugged. "If we get enough rain, I could just go and stand out in the clearing as bait."

"That's not funny."

He smirked. "It kinda was."

I smiled and finished the last mouthful of my rice. At least he'd almost smiled; it was a start.

He sighed and stirred his rice a bit before pushing it away in disgust.

"Sick of my cooking already?"

I was aiming for funny, but he blinked, wide eyed. "Oh no, not at all. I'm just not that hungry. Sorry."

"It's okay. There's only so many days you can eat spicy rice."

"I actually really like this," he said. Then he frowned. "I wish I didn't have to leave. I wish I could stay here. Just us two." Then he cringed. "Or just me, if that sounded a bit presumptuous. I just . . ." He sighed. "It's just being here with you, with no responsibility, no outside world. Just chasing the storms, doing what we want when we want, and . . ."

"And having great sex," I finished for him.

He blushed, his smile shy. "It's been the best time of my life," he admitted, his blue eyes deep as the ocean. "That probably sounds lame to you, but this?" He gestured to the bunker, then to me. "This doesn't happen to guys like me."

"What do you mean guys like you?"

"Nerd. Loner. Weirdo. Freak. I believe there's a list."

"You mean smart and sexy, with cojones the size of basketballs."

He gawped, then felt his crotch. "What?"

"Not literally." I chuckled. "Metaphorically speaking. You have balls of steel. Fearless."

His smiled twisted and he frowned. "I was scared today. And yesterday," he whispered. "For you. I was scared for you. That I'd put you in danger, and I'm sorry I did that."

"You didn't make me do anything."

"Actually, I kinda did. I said I would just take your Jeep and go to the mangroves without you if you didn't want to come."

I chuckled. "I already added stubborn to the smart and sexy list."

He chewed on the inside of his lip for a few moments. "Thank you for bringing me out here," he said, meeting my gaze once more. "I know I cut into your time off, and having to babysit me mustn't have been your idea of fun."

"Are you kidding? I've had the best time! You're forgettin' that this is what I do. I'd be here regardless, if you were with me or not. Storm chaser, remember? And the company's been great. I've really enjoyed having you here. Plus, the sex has been amazing."

He blushed again and played with his fingers. "I just want you to know I'm grateful, that's all."

"You're welcome. Maybe next time you come out here, one of us will remember condoms so we settle that 'who's a top' argument once and for all."

He laughed then. "I'll try to remember."

"I won't forget, believe me."

He scooted off the bed, collected the bowls, and took them to the sink. "Thank you again for dinner."

I watched him as he began to wash up, then I walked over and leaned against the counter. "So, about tomorrow."

"What about it?"

"We should pack up tonight, so in the morning we'll have breakfast, load up the Jeep and we can go."

He nodded solemnly. "Sounds good."

I took the tea towel and began to dry. "So, where are you staying in Darwin?"

He glanced at me, confused. "I'm not."

"Oh, it's just that given we're leaving here two days

early," I said. "I wondered if you had somewhere to stay. When's your flight?"

He baulked. "Oh. I hadn't thought of that." He shook his head, mad at himself. "I'll see if the airline can amend my booking. I'm sure I have a flexible ticket." He grimaced. "I hope it is, at least."

"You can stay with me," I offered, aiming for casual, feeling anything but. "I'm still off work so I'm not expected to be anywhere. I can play tour guide in Darwin instead of here, if you want. My place is big enough. I have a spare room if you're sick of sharing with me, and—" I waggled my eyebrows at him. "I have a decent supply of condoms and lube."

His whole face went red, not even the tops of his ears were safe. He stared at the bubbles in the sink. "Oh, uh . . ."

He was considering it, I could tell. He didn't want to say no, he just wasn't sure if he should say yes. I had to strike while the iron was hot.

"And we should take your gear to the bureau office in Darwin."

That made him look at me. "What for?"

"To check the data box and run your laptop, see if it survived the power surge. They'll have the equipment to download your information. So you know what you've got before you get back to Melbourne." I had no idea if that was what meteorologists in the field did, but it sounded good to me. "I dunno," I added. "Is that what smart and sexy science guys do?"

He fought a smile. "Are you asking me to stay with you until my scheduled flight?"

He was absolutely staying.

"Damn right I am. More storms, more science-y stuff, and more sex. What's not to like?"

He grinned then. "Okay."

PACKIN' up the Jeep and locking up the bunker felt really final. Like we were leavin' something behind. Not any physical thing, but maybe a part of myself.

I'd never brought anyone special to the bunker before, and now I wasn't sure I ever wanted to come back alone.

Now that I knew how good it could be to share it with someone.

I emptied the last of the jerry can of petrol into the Jeep and jumped in behind the driver's seat. The rain was still coming down steadily and I had to shake my hair like a dog, just for good measure.

Jeremiah gave me a shove. "Ugh."

He wiped his face melodramatically as I started the engine. "You ready?"

"Not really. How bad will these roads be?"

"Drivable," I answered. "But if we leave it any longer, we'd need a hovercraft."

He sighed. "You said every road we've been on was drivable. I can assure you, we have differing opinions on what is drivable."

"It won't be so bad," I said, trying to help him relax. "We just gotta outrun the rain."

I grinned and began the slow drive out. The road out was wet and slippery, and I didn't want to risk putting us in a ditch. The rain was constant and heavy, dangerous even. We probably should have left yesterday after the storm.

"I guess I should be grateful you put the roof on," he said, one hand on the oh-shit bar as we bounced down into one particularly rough part.

"You hate it now," I said. "But you'll miss this."

He shot me a glare that was half 'I absolutely will not' and half 'shut up I know I will.'

At the fork in the track, this time we turned right. We'd gone left to the mangroves and we could see now that all that area to the west was now *very* swampy.

"Oh god. Is that where we were?"

I nodded. "Ten kilometres further into that."

"Jesus," he whispered. "I'd have died out here for sure."

I laughed. "That's why you have me. So maybe next time when I say, 'hey, it's not a good idea to go into the mangroves at this time of year,' you might listen. Because when it comes to being out here, I'm the expert."

I just then happened to hit a very large, very deep, very wet pothole, and we bounced so hard we both almost hit our heads on the roof.

He held on with two hands and shot me a harrowed look. "You were saying?"

IT STILL RAINED, but the further southeast we went, the better the track became until we turned onto an actual road. And the sadder it made me. I didn't want my time with him to be over, and every mile we drove, it felt like we were leaving our time together behind us.

Sure, he'd agreed to another two days in Darwin. But being out here at the bunker with him had been special, and it was only when we were leaving that I truly realised that.

When we'd reached a tarred road, the rain had eased, and Jeremiah asked me to pull the Jeep over. "Why?"

"I want to roll the top back," he said with a grin. "If I have two more days of freedom, I want to feel it."

So we rolled the roof back, and as we drove back toward civilisation, through the ancient green forests of Kakadu, the wind tousled our hair and Jeremiah put his hands up into the wind and laughed.

Yeah. I was going to miss him so fucking much.

CHAPTER FOURTEEN

JEREMIAH

WE REFUELLED IN JABIRU, AND I MET TULLY AT THE counter of the service station. "You two made it out before the rains," the man behind the counter said. "Was wondering how you were gettin' on out there."

"Sad to cut it short this trip," Tully said.

I was quick to add a bottle of Coke and some snacks to Tully's fuel total and he grinned at me. "Anything else?"

I shook my head. "Unless you want something."

He looked at the lollies and Pringles. "I'm having half of that."

I rolled my eyes, took my stash, and the man serving us laughed. "See you boys again soon."

Yes, well, as much I wished otherwise, that wasn't likely. I nodded all the same and went back to the Jeep. I understood now why all the cool kids would drive with the tops down on their cars. The feel of the wind in my hair felt like freedom. Sitting next to Tully, having him laugh and wear that damn grin, aiming it right at me . . . it was the closest to real happiness I'd ever felt in my life. Care-free, all while being the real me.

I'd never shared the real me with anyone before. Just him. And that time was slowly ticking down to an end.

As we got closer to Darwin, as the traffic filled in around us, as the greenery became farms and then houses, I couldn't help feeling a little sad.

"Have you been to Darwin before?" Tully asked.

"Just the airport, for one hour, then I flew into Jabiru and met you."

"I'll show you around," he said, leaning over and taking my hand. He brought it to his thigh, leaving it there, smiling at my surprise. He kept his hand on mine, unless he had to change gears, but he was quick to grab it again, squeezing, slipping his fingers through mine.

It both thrilled me and made my heart ache.

Why couldn't I find this in my real life?

Why did something so perfect have to end?

I tried to push those intrusive thoughts away, until we were in the centre of Darwin and I realised, stupidly late, that the streets we drove down were very nice. Huge houses, new and perfectly neat and tidy, expensive cars and palm trees, and . . .

And he slowed down at a driveway, the automatic gate to the property sliding open. He drove in, the garage door opened, and he parked next to a very expensive Range Rover.

He opened his door, got out, and stretched his arms up high with a loud yawn. "Are you getting out?"

I wasn't sure if I should.

"Is this . . . do you live here?"

He looked around, confused. "Ah yeah? This is my house. Well, mine and the bank's."

It had white rendered walls, and even the garage was spotlessly clean. And the car . . . "Uh, is this yours too?" I pointed my chin at the Range Rover.

"Yep. The company leases them. I get a new one every two years."

Must be nice.

"Cool."

He shrugged, like it was no big deal. "Let's unpack the Jeep first. Get all the shit out and dump our bags straight into the laundry." He opened the tailgate and pulled out my crate of equipment, gently placing it by the door that I assumed went into the house. He carried the box of left-over food. I grabbed both our bags and followed him inside.

We entered in through what I quickly realised was a laundry room. Except it was almost the size of my entire apartment. The floor was dark, the cabinetry all gloss white, a full counter top and cupboards.

"Just throw 'em in here," he said, indicating to our bags. "We'll need to wash everything."

I propped them by the washing machine and followed him into the rest of the house. It was massive, open plan, double storey. The walls were white, the floor a dark grey marble, the furniture was straight from a designer, and the kitchen was ridiculously luxurious. There was white glossy cabinetry and a dark grey stone benchtop that opened out to the lounge room with a sofa setting that looked as comfortable as it looked expensive. But none of that was even the best part. Because there were glass doors that led out to a balcony and, sure enough, it looked straight out over the ocean.

Was he kidding me right now?

He slid the box onto the countertop and opened one cupboard door—which I realised was a built-in fridge. Jeez.

He unloaded the canned goods into his butler's pantry and put the box on the floor. "Come on, I'll give you a tour."

"There's more?"

He laughed and led the way upstairs. "Spare room," he said, pointing at one door. "Another spare room. Bathroom through there. And this," he said, opening a door at the end of the hall, "is my room."

It was huge, and it had its own balcony. Everything was huge. The room, the bed, the walk-in wardrobe, the ensuite, and for a second I had a hard time marrying this house to the guy I'd just spent days with roughing it in the tropical jungle, staying in a tin shed, and driving an old beaten-up Jeep. I wasn't sure how they could be the same person . . .

But then I noticed the framed photographs on the wall. I mean, they too looked like they belonged in a museum, black frames all artfully displayed. But they were black and white photos of storms.

Rain clouds and lightning.

He stood beside me. "I took those photos," he said quietly, and we both studied each image.

I got closer to one, pointing to it. "That's the bunker."

"Sure is." He slung his arm over my shoulder, effectively tucking me under his arm, and pointed up to another photo. "And that one. And this one. Can't see the shed at all, but that's the clearing looking east. It's a few years old so the trees look a bit different."

"I love these pictures," I whispered. "I was beginning to think this wasn't your house."

He pulled back so he could look into my eyes. "What do you mean?"

I shrugged. "This is all very extravagant and luxurious, and the you I know just spent a week running around in the jungle without a shirt or shoes in a banged-up Jeep."

He smiled and took my hand, bringing my palm to his cheek, and he closed his eyes. "That's who I am," he murmured. His brown eyes met mine. "Out there, where I have no expectations or obligations. Here?" he said, looking around the room. "You think this is all glamour, but it's not really. I mean, it is. I know I'm privileged to have this. I know that. So yeah, this is also me, but this me is where real life takes the shine off who I am." He dropped my hand and frowned. "Don't get me wrong. I'm not cryin' poor little rich boy, but who I was with you this last week was the me no one else gets to see."

Oh wow. Okay, I wasn't expecting such heartfelt honesty. And I wasn't expecting him to echo my thoughts so completely.

I put my hand to his chest. "Who I was this last week with you was the real me too. The me that no one else understands. Or likes."

The corner of his mouth pulled up in a half-smile, and he put his finger to my chin, bringing me in for a soft kiss. "I like you."

CHAPTER FIFTEEN

TULLY

I GAVE JEREMIAH SOME SHORTS AND A SHIRT FROM my wardrobe and handed him a clean towel. "Come downstairs when you're done."

"Oh, I need my shaving kit."

I rubbed my thumb along his scruffy jaw and hummed. "Or you could leave it."

I wanted nothin' more than to get into the shower with him, and I almost did, but getting cleaned up after a week of camping was a solitary thing. Sure, the shower at the bunker was adequate, but here he had proper hot water, shower gel, and a flushing toilet.

I left him to it and went downstairs. I upended my bag of dirty clothes into the washing machine and put in a quick grocery order for some essentials, and I'd just finished ordering some pizza when Jeremiah came down the stairs.

"Hm," I said appreciatively. "I like you in my clothes. Did you notice that I didn't give you any underwear?"

He rolled his eyes but he did smile. "That was the best shower I've ever had."

"Which is why I didn't join you," I said. His mouth fell open and I shrugged. "I thought about it. I almost did. I *really* wanted to. But that first shower when you get back . . ." I held his chin. "And you left the scruff."

"Yes, well, I didn't have a razor."

My eyes fell to his lips, his very kissable lips, and god, he smelled so good. I groaned and took a step back. "I want to do unholy things to you right now, but I need to get myself cleaned up first." I headed for the stairs. "The AC's on. I've ordered pizza. Help yourself to anything in the fridge."

I took the stairs two at a time to put some distance between us. I wanted to drag him to bed, but god, considering how good and clean he smelled, I must have stunk like a sweaty horse. Takin' him to bed like this would be gross and insulting. I intended to have the quickest shower of my life until I felt the hot water on my skin. I scrubbed my hair, lathered up soap over every inch of my body, then did it all again.

I felt decidedly more human when I went downstairs, and excited. We'd talked about having sex when we got here, now that we had condoms and lube, and I was keen to know if that was still on the table. I found the glass doors open and Jeremiah was taking in the view.

"You like it?" I asked.

He turned when I spoke and smiled. "I've never seen the Timor Sea before."

"Technically this is Beagle Gulf, and the Timor Sea is a bit further out," I said.

"Can we go for a swim at the beach?" He asked. "Because it's hot as hell."

I made a face. He'd said before he liked to swim. "Uh, well, you can," I said. "But it's not exactly recommended. We get the occasional crocodile, and the Irukandji jellyfish—"

He put his hand up. "I'm sorry I asked."

"But it is about twenty degrees cooler inside if you'd prefer to look at the pretty, unswimmable water from the other side of the glass door. You know, where there is air conditioning."

He smiled, squinting one eye at the sun. "You can't really get the whole Top End 'baked and steamed at the same time' experience from inside though."

"Baked *and* steamed, huh?"

"I feel like a dumpling."

I laughed and went to the door, waiting for him to walk in first. "They call it the silly season here," I explained. "This weather, the oven and sauna effect, it makes people do silly things."

"Like choose to live here?"

I went to the fridge, took out two beers, and handed him one. "You get used to it."

He looked at the beer, then looked at me. "I generally don't drink a great deal, so unless you're getting me drunk to take advantage of me."

I grinned at him. "I was hoping you'd bring that up because—"

The intercom buzzed.

"Goddammit," I said, putting my beer down. "That'll be the pizza."

I took the delivery and put the pizzas on the coffee table. "Let's eat here," I said, collecting my beer and waiting for him to join me on the couch.

"This is the biggest couch I've ever seen." He sat down. "And the softest."

It was big. I bought it because it was deep and pillowy. "So easy to fall asleep on this thing. I'll be watching TV and then the next thing I know, it's 3:00 am."

He chuckled but made a face. "Is it okay to eat on here?"

"Hell yeah. Why wouldn't it be?"

"Because it's . . ."

"It's my house. I eat all my meals here, or standin' at the kitchen counter. I spilled nachos on this couch *the day* I got it." I opened the pizza box and handed him the first slice. "I'm not the pretentious fancy type."

He smiled, but it soon became a grimace. "Sorry. I don't mean to judge. I've just never been in a house this nice before. I wasn't sure what I should touch."

"Touch anything you want. Including me." I took a bite of my pizza. Then, like the uncouth monster I was, I spoke with my mouth full. "Hope you like supreme."

He laughed and, like a gentleman, chewed and swallowed before he spoke. "It's great, thanks."

I waited until I'd swallowed before I spoke again. "I get it, though. Honestly, my eldest brother and sister are the pretentious type. They're the real serious ones, serious about the business. It's all about the money to them. They name-drop and do the snobby pouty faces when something's beneath them. Which is weird because my parents aren't like that. They earned their money, and they were normal before they got rich. My brother and sister grew up rich and feel entitled, or something, I dunno." Then I felt bad for saying that. "Well, that's not true, really. They work hard and they shoulder a lot of the responsibility. But they look down at me because I chase storms for fun when their idea of time off is to read *Business Insider*. Know what I mean? We're just very different. So yeah, people who live like this can be pretentious and think they're better than others. Rowan and Zoe are proof of that."

Jeremiah made a face. "I'm sorry. I didn't mean to assume. This is just . . . it's not a world I'm familiar with." He sipped his beer. "When I say I grew up poor, I mean it. Some days we ate, some days we didn't. My dad worked very hard."

Oh man.

"I'm sorry," I said. "And more often than not, the degree to which someone works is not indicative of their pay grade. Half the CEOs of the world couldn't do what their employees do. They wouldn't last half a day doin' manual labour, and it's those workers who make the world turn." I took another bite of pizza. "That's why you find me with the cooks and ground staff at our docks. I'm more comfortable with them than I am at those fancy dinners my brother and sister go to. But if the bosses need to know what's really going on or what needs to be done, or what's not being done properly, or what issues the workers are havin' at the ground level, they come to me." I shook my head, unsure why I was telling him this. "Sorry. I just don't want you to think I'm like them."

His eyes met mine, kind and warm. "I don't. And I like

that you understand." We ate some more pizza, and he took another mouthful of beer, almost drainin' his bottle. "Now, this may be the beer talking, because I haven't drunk alcohol in over a year, but about that offer to touch anything I want."

I grinned at him, downed the rest of my beer, took his hand, and led him upstairs.

And we'd hinted and joked about which of us would top, but there was never any doubt. He pulled my shirt off and tossed it, his eyes dark, and he licked his lips. "Get on the bed."

That look, those words, almost set my blood on fire.

I quickly complied, scooting into the middle, my head on the pillows. I pointed to the bedside table. "Top drawer."

He found the condoms and lube, throwing them onto the bed beside me, then pulled off his shirt and knelt on the mattress, crawlin' over to me. He planted himself between my legs and slid his hands up my thighs, over my hips to the waistband of my shorts. He smirked as he pulled them down, like this was the victory he'd wanted.

He leaned forward so he could kiss me, soft, open lips, and the hint of tongue. "I want to kiss you," he murmured. Those blue eyes were like fucking fire. "Then I'm going to suck your cock and eat your arse before I fuck you."

My body felt hot all over, my brain short circuited. I think I groaned. "Fuck."

Who was this guy?

"When I said you gave me top vibes, I didn't expect this."

He sucked my bottom lip in between his. "Want me to take it easy on you?"

I grinned at him, trying to get his shorts off. "Hell no."

He took my wrists in his hands and pinned them beside my head. "Can I ask you something?"

I was almost panting with need. "Yes."

"Have you ever had a prostate orgasm?"

Jesus fucking Christ.

It took me a second to think, to breathe. "No," I whispered.

He grinned. "You will tonight."

I don't know why I was so stunned. Thinkin' back to what we'd done in the bunker, and the way he'd pulled my hair, how he'd held my face when he slid his cock into my throat, I should have known.

This quiet science nerd had a freaky side.

Hell fucking yes.

He kissed me then, tanglin' his tongue with mine until I forgot my own name. He moulded me with his mouth, with his hands, the perfect combination of gentle and rough, and his body against mine until I was pliable and desperate.

Then he flipped me over, massaged my back, kissed up my spine, and bit my shoulder; an ebb and flow of pleasure and pain. He rid me of my shorts and splayed me open, delving his tongue inside me.

I gripped my bed covers and lifted my hips for him, and he worked me harder. First with his tongue, then with his fingers and lube, fingering me and stretching. Feeling . . .

Until he found his prize.

"Holy shit," I gasped, coming up on all fours.

"Hm," he purred. "There it is."

With his fingers still inside me, he pushed my head back down with his other hand so my arse was in the air. And he pressed against my prostate again and again, sparking a pleasure inside me like nothin' I'd ever felt before.

"God, right there, don't stop," I mumbled. It was so intense I could have cried. I was prepared to beg for this to never end. Then he wrapped his hand around my cock and began to stroke, and it was too much pleasure. It was sensory overload and obliterated every synapse in my body, and I needed him to make it end but also to please, never stop. "Fuck, Jeremiah," I cried, almost a sob. "Please."

Please, what? I wasn't sure.

Finish me, make me come, please please, never stop, I need this forever, I can't take anymore, god please . . .

Pleasure was overwhelming, so consuming, it bordered on pain, until the build-up was too much. An orgasm so powerful it felt like I exploded and imploded at the same time. I screamed into my mattress, my voice hoarse, my hands were claws in the bedding.

I was shaking and groaning, the ultimate fucking high . . . until I collapsed in a heap.

I'd been obliterated.

It took a few minutes for my senses to come back to me. I was still shaking, my body trembling, muscles convulsing.

Jeremiah pulled the cover over me and kissed the side of my head. "Are you okay?"

I wanted to say no and yes, but it came out as a laugh.

"The fuck did you do to me?" I managed to say. My voice sounded weird. "Imma need you to do it again."

He chuckled and I focused on him then. He looked so happy, so sexy, my god, so sexy . . . but he still had shorts on—and I could see his erection confined in them. "You didn't . . ."

His smile became a grin. "I haven't finished with you yet."

I shivered and another tremor racked through me. My words came out in a groan. "Oh god."

He laughed as he rolled off the bed. He went into the bathroom and used mouthwash, came back out with a cloth to clean me up, and he did let me recover. Somewhat.

For about an hour, he massaged me, skimmin' my body with his hands as if he was mappin' me out. He peppered soft kisses all over me, rubbing me down, and I was so relaxed by the time he rolled a condom on, all I could do was smile into my pillow.

Face down, arse up, he knelt behind me, added more lube, and slowly pressed into me. "Oh fuck," I groaned into my pillow.

He was slow and thorough, pushing in to the hilt, then pressing his weight onto my back. He kissed my spine, my nape, his breaths short and sharp, shaking with his restraint.

So I moved my hips, pushing back on his cock, and he took it as permission to move.

He pulled back and pushed back in, slow and deep. He slid his hands over mine, threading our fingers, his breaths and grunts hot on the back of my neck and in my ear. "You feel so good," he moaned.

I pressed my forehead into the pillow, trying to stretch my back, my hips pinned to the bed. Then he pulled out of me and flipped me over, bringing my legs over his thighs, he bent me in half and sunk back into me as he sunk his tongue into my mouth.

Oh dear god.

He whined, a low guttural sound, and his grip on my hips tightened. He thrust harder and deeper until he gasped and cried out as he came.

I held his face and watched as those blue eyes melted, liquid sapphires lost to his own pleasure.

It was fucking beautiful.

My god, this man . . .

How was I ever going to let him leave the day after tomorrow?

I traced patterns on his back until he could lift his own head. He plonked his cheek onto his palm with a goofy, sleepy smile, and he looked kinda drunk. It made me laugh. "Yeah, so," I said. "About you leavin' in two days. How are you going to do the prostate thing once a week when you're in Melbourne and I'm here?"

He raised one eyebrow. "Just once a week?"

"Pretty sure that's all I could handle."

He smiled, kissed me one more time, then rolled out of bed. We played clean up and got redressed and went in search of our now-cold pizza.

Jeremiah stopped at the glass doors. "Oh wow," he said, looking out at the horizon.

I chuckled. It was a brilliant array of orange, reds, yellows, all reflecting off pillows of dark clouds. "Ah, the famous Darwin sunset. Pretty, huh?"

"There's a warm updraft rolling in. There'll be lightning for sure."

I took the pizza and opened the sliding door. "Then let's go watch the show."

It was hot outside, even as the sun was setting, but the sheen of sweat on Jeremiah's skin made it worthwhile. The colours of the sunset and the threatening storm made him look even more beautiful.

"Want another beer?" I asked.

"Uh, sure," he replied, just as his phone beeped. He'd had a few messages, which he'd groaned at and ignored, but this time he sighed. "It's my boss. Telling me to ignore the earlier messages because they've just realised that I'm not in the office. After a week, mind you." His eyes met mine. "Can we go back to the middle of nowhere where there's no phone service? Or should I just lob this into the ocean?" He held his phone as if about to throw it.

I grabbed his hand and put it around my waist, leaning against him and giving him a soft kiss. "So don't go back."

He rolled his eyes. "While that sounds all good and well, I believe reality beckons."

I lifted his chin, brushing my nose against his. "What awaits you in Melbourne?" I kissed his lips, down his jaw. "A job you hate."

"A job I love, work colleagues I hate." His breath caught when I bit his earlobe. "My father."

That made me pause. I sighed and pulled away. "Yeah, sorry. I forgot. I just . . . I just don't want our time together to end just yet."

He studied my eyes, searching for something. "I'm trying to decide if you're pranking me. My dating history would tell me yes, but then you seem so sincere. I'd like to think you're different . . ."

I sighed, reining in my temper because his knee-jerk reaction to being ridiculed wasn't about me.

"Jeremiah," I murmured. "I am sincere. And clearly I am different to the arseholes you've dated before. I'm sorry they made you doubt me."

"It's not you," he said apologetically.

"I know."

"But . . ." He ran his hand through his hair, then used it to wave me up and down. "But you're perfect. Gorgeous, rich, successful. And I'm . . ."

"You're what?"

"Me."

"You," I said, pointing my finger and lightly jabbing him in the chest with every point I made. "You who earned a doctorate probably a decade sooner than any of the pricks you work with. You, who shows absolutely zero fear. You, with the bluest blue eyes that give me butterflies. And you, who earlier ate my arse and gave me the best orgasm of my life. That same you?"

He almost smiled, clearly not very adept at taking compliments. "The best orgasm, huh?"

"Uncontested." I ran my hand over his heart, up to his jaw, and made him look at me. "What you did to me earlier? It's no wonder I want you to stay. Honestly, if you do go back to Melbourne, I might have to come visit a few times a year just so you can do it again."

He chuckled, his eyes warm. Then licked his lips, wincing, and turned to the ocean. "Lightning."

And sure enough, the clouds over the bay lit up. A

deafening crack of thunder ripped through the sky, and while most normal people would have run for cover, Jeremiah turned to face it. Several bolts of lightning hit the water, less than a kilometre away. Furious and frightening, the storm broke and rain poured.

Jeremiah smiled.

CHAPTER SIXTEEN

JEREMIAH

"Hi, Dad. It's me," I said, my phone to my ear. I was standing at the glass doors overlooking the ocean, only from inside where it was air conditioned, because this Darwin heat was no joke. Even at 8:00 am. I'd left Tully in the shower upstairs, and I could hear him singing from where I was. Maybe the hand job after breakfast made him too happy . . .

"I was wondering when I'd hear from you. How's your trip?"

"Yeah, it's great. Back in Darwin now. Had no phone service all week, sorry."

"You get what you were after?"

I thought about my gear, how the recording unit was probably fried, how this whole trip was probably for naught, and I considered launching into an explanation my father wouldn't care about . . . but then Tully began a very loud rendition of 'Sex on Fire' and I smiled. "Yeah. I think so, Dad. I'm heading into the Darwin office this morning."

"Okay. You back tomorrow, right?"

I withheld a sigh, because going back to my shitty life in Melbourne was the last thing I wanted to do. "Yeah. I'll call you when I get in."

"Right then. I better get back to work. You're in a different time zone to me, ya know."

"Yeah, Dad. I know."

The line went quiet in my ear, just as Tully came skipping down the stairs. He was grinning until he saw me. "Oh, what's up?"

"Nothing. Just spoke to my dad."

"Everything okay?"

Not really. "Yep. Same as always."

Tully watched me for a second and thankfully dropped it. "You ready to go?"

"Yep. My equipment crate is in the garage. I'm ready to see if it's all completely fried and all my work is gone."

He slung his arm over my shoulder and led me toward the garage. "It'll be fine, just you wait and see."

I envied his optimism.

In the garage, I lifted the crate and carried it to the back of the Jeep, but Tully opened the back of the Range Rover instead. "Today we go in style."

I frowned. "Uh, the Jeep is more my style."

He laughed and helped me slide the crate into his new car and I already had to wipe my brow. "I have two words for you," he said. "Air. Conditioning." Then he walked to the passenger door and opened it for me. "Your chariot, sire."

I rolled my eyes but got in, and yes, the newer car was amazing and very fancy, and I'd have been perfectly happy in the Jeep, but yes, the air conditioning was very much appreciated.

He drove me along the shoreline, pointing out things of interest. "This whole marina is new," he said. "There's cafés and restaurants. We can have dinner there tonight if you want. All the trees have lights and it's really pretty."

I nodded, trying not to think that it'd be our last night together. "Sounds good."

He pointed out more landmarks as he drove us out of the city centre, through some back streets, until we eventually got to our destination. The Darwin meteorology station was a small blond brick building sitting in the middle of a large dirt block, fenced off and not inviting at all. Built in the 1970s, by the looks of it, and not updated since.

But the gate was open and a motorbike with a sidecar was parked under the shelter at the side of the building.

I'd had very limited dealings with this Darwin office— this was the station, not the admin office—and I really had no idea of who or what to expect.

"Have you met Doreen before?" Tully asked.

"Uh, no. Have you?"

"I had to pick up some gear a time or two and take it out to the Jabiru Airport. Someone told her I was headed out there." He grinned at me. "She's a bit different."

"I have no issue with different." Before I could ask if the motorbike was hers, a figure came through the front door with a baseball bat. Big and tall, shaved head, black jeans and a black singlet top with 'Vagitarian: I eat pussy' written in pink across the front. She was late sixties, maybe seventies. Big boobs, menacing snarl.

"You got no business here," she said, pointing the baseball bat at us.

"Oh my god," I hissed, clutching at my seatbelt. "Tully, turn the car around!"

Tully laughed and got out. "Calm down, woman. Jesus Christ," he said with his disarming grin. "Love your shirt."

Oh my god! He did not just call her *woman*!

We were both about to die . . .

She lowered the bat and relented a smile. "Tully. Whatcha hidin' that good-looking head of yours in those tinted windows for? Dumbass, I almost took m'bat to your fancy car."

Tully gave me a nod, silently telling me to get my arse out of the car. "Brought someone to see ya."

He shut his door and walked over to her, turned, and waited for me to get out, which I did. Still unsure if we were about to die . . .

"Doreen, this is Doctor Jeremiah Overton. From the Melbourne office."

She eyed me. "Who's your boss?"

"Brian Carling."

She gave a nod. "Got your ID card on ya?"

In a panic, I fumbled my wallet, barely managing to hand her the card. She studied it, then me. "Doctor, huh?"

"Yes."

A slow smile spread across her hardened face. "Why didn't ya say that?" she said, grabbing my hand and shaking it, almost rattling the teeth in my head. "Come on inside."

I wasn't led in so much as accosted through the door, and I was too terrified to not comply. There was a small entry hall with a plastic plant, and a door that led through to a dark room where one wall was lined with radar, sonars, screens, and flashing lights, the other wall was lined with shelves full of gear. Old anemometers, a tripod, a machine that looked like a hygrometer from the '60s; boxes of gear that belonged in a museum.

Jesus. How old was this place?

"Here's the bridge," she said, as if this was some ship that needed steering. Every single panel was something from the '90s. Oh my god, it was older than me. Doreen must have noticed my face.

"Bet it's nothin' fancy like you're used to. She's old, but she ain't ever stopped."

The old air conditioning unit rattled and clunked, scaring me, and Doreen walked over to it and walloped it with the heel of her hand, which scared me even more. I was surprised it stayed on the wall, let alone kicked into gear.

Then something yipped and I almost jumped out of my skin until Doreen scooped up a small poodle-looking thing off the one and only seat in the entire room.

"This is Bruce," she said. "Not scared of a little dog, are ya?"

Before I could answer—words were failing me right at that minute—Tully was behind me, holding my crate. "He ain't scared of anything," he said with a smirk. He put my crate down. "Well, maybe an amphibian or two, but a fifty-thousand-volt lightning strike don't faze him at all."

I was beginning to think I'd walked into a time warp. How was this station still operational?

"I gotta say," Doreen said. "I'm surprised to see ya. I didn't think anyone was ever comin'."

I was still trying to get my head around any single thing that had happened in the last three minutes.

"Uh, my automatic weather station was taken out in a storm two days ago, and a power surge took out my hard drive," I said. "I was hoping I could use your system to see if anything's retrievable. I'd hate to think all my data is lost." I looked at the console unit, doubting anything was compatible for me to use. Not without a time machine.

Doreen fished her keys from her pocket, and putting Bruce back on the seat, she unthreaded some keys and handed them to me. "I don't give one fuck what you do, kid."

Uh . . .

Um . . .

"P-p-pardon?"

"You're my replacement, right?" she picked up a pink biker helmet and put it on, then nodded to the keys in the palm of my hand. "Keys. There's only two. Front door, front gate. Lock 'em both when you leave."

I shook my head, confused. Bewildered. "What?"

She picked Bruce up. "I retired six months ago, been waitin' on my replacement for-fucking-ever. Arsehats in Sydney kept tellin' me there was no one. Guess it was Melbourne who come through for me. Always did like Melbourne, though that Brian's a bit of a knob."

I shook my head and held out the keys she'd handed me. "No, no, there's been some kind of mistake," I tried.

"Air con's been dying for five years," she said. "A good kick in the ribs usually gets it goin'."

"Doreen, there seems—"

"I'll leave ya the bat by the door," she said. "Sometimes the local kids think they need an antenna off the roof. Whatever's in the fridge is yours. I'm outta here. I've been here since Tracy."

I looked at Tully, bewildered. *Who the hell was Tracy?*

"Cyclone Tracy," he murmured.

Oh.

Panic was starting to bubble in my chest. "I just wanted to calibrate—"

Doreen clapped me on the shoulder so hard I fell into Tully. "Congrats on the job," she said. "Hope you don't like co-workers or budgets, cause you ain't got either."

And with that, she was gone. The door banged as she left, a second later her motorbike rumbled to life and by the time I thought to chase after her, all we got was a wave as she took off out the gate, Bruce sitting up in the sidecar with dog-goggles on.

And I stood there with my mouth hanging open and a set of keys in my hand.

I turned to Tully, dumbfounded. "Wh-what the hell . . ." I held the keys on the palm of my hand as if they'd just landed from outer space. "What just happened?"

Tully pressed his lips together so he didn't smile too hard, but his eyes were full of humour. "I think you just got a promotion?"

I shook my head, my mind reeling. "That's not . . . I can't . . . what the . . ."

"Yeah, look," he said with a shrug. "I ain't mad about it. There's a saying about gift horses or something."

"Tully! I live and work in Melbourne!"

He made a face, glanced pointedly at the keys, and clicked his tongue. "Well, I'm thinkin' that's not exactly true." Then he winced. "Anymore."

A beeping noise began blaring inside. "What the hell is that?"

We raced inside. One of the small warning lights was flashing yellow.

"I dunno," Tully said. "This gear is your domain."

"This gear is older than me," I said. "I don't know how any of this works."

"Flip some switches," he said, flipping the old metal switches that did god-only knows what. "Make the noise stop."

"You can't just flip—"

The beeping stopped.

Jesus H Christ.

I looked at the screen. It was a radar, and there was a mass of orange and purple blinking in and out of view. It was old, yes, but I knew what that meant. "Storm front moving in from the north. I think it's a low-pressure warning system. It's gonna be decent."

Tully looked at me, grinning.

"Don't smile at me," I said, taking my phone out and calling my boss. I held my phone to my ear and began to check the other equipment. "Come on, answer your damn phone—"

"Overton," he said, grumpily. "You finally replying to the messages I left for you."

"How long was it until you realised I was on annual leave?"

Silence.

Maybe he still hadn't realised.

He grumbled something I couldn't hear. "What do you want? This better be good."

I scoffed. "I'll give you good. I've just been handed the keys to the Darwin station. The woman that gave them to me quit, or finally retired, I don't even know. The equipment here is from the '90s. Hell, there's an anemometer so old I think it came off the Endeavour. Do you hear what I'm saying? I can't work here. I never agreed to work here. I came here this morning to see if I could use the in house system to recalibrate my gear and maybe save some of the data I collected that got fried from when we got *struck by lightning* in the middle of the damn jungle, but I can now see that was an exercise in futility because the computer system here is straight out of a time machine, and you'll have to excuse my language but it's so fucking damn hot here my brain is melting!"

There was a long beat of silence. "What the hell are you talking about, Overton?"

"Brian, listen to me," I said through clenched teeth. "What you're gonna do is find out what the fuck is going on. Call Sydney, call Canberra. Call the fucking prime minister if you have to. Get Doreen back here, today, and find out who the hell is the replacement officer up here."

"Who's Doreen?"

"She's the six-foot woman with a shaved head and a baseball bat that just gave me her keys to the Darwin station, that's who! Now get off your arse and start making phone calls!"

I disconnected the call, my chest heaving. "The incompetence," I muttered.

Tully took my hand, grinning. "You're awesome, you know that?"

My head was swimming and my vision blurred. Tully put me in Bruce's seat and patted my cheek. "You okay?"

I shook my head. "I just wanted to check my data."

"I know," he said.

Fucker was still smiling.

"Glad you find this whole situation amusing."

He laughed, now on his knees before me, and cupped my face. "Are you okay?"

I shook my head and shrugged. I had no clue what I was.

"You bein' all kickass to your boss just now was really hot."

I sagged, burying my face in my hands. "I'm so fired."

Just then, the radar began to beep again. With a heavy sigh, I began to look at the instruments, the equipment. "I feel like I'm in a movie, you know when a modern-day pilot has to fly a plane from the 1940s or something and the whole dash is full of buttons that don't make sense." I shook my head, starting to think a little clearer. "That's an early Doppler and this is a RAPIC, I think. I've seen them in pictures."

Tully squeezed my shoulder. "See? You're getting it already."

I flipped the switches back on that he'd shut off earlier. I wheeled my chair over to the right. "And this is one of the first time-lapse sequencers. My god, did we *go* back in time?"

"Kinda feels like it."

"Can you please do me a favour and see if there's a manual or instruction booklet on the shelves or in a cupboard, or—" I looked around. "—something, somewhere. A filing cabinet, maybe. Google won't help me here."

Tully went straight to the shelves and started lifting things and rummaging through boxes. I turned back once to see that he'd found a helmet with a torchlight strapped to it. It was now on his head. By the time I'd read the old printed labels underneath some metal flip switches and correlated it to its function on the dash, Tully let out a loud, "Ta-da!" while wielding a book over his helmet.

"Printed in 1992," he said, handing it over.

It was, indeed, a manual to the instrument dash. From 1992.

"Oh god," I said, taking the book. I dusted it off and skimmed through the first pages. The radar beeped again, and at least I knew which switch to flip. The storm was still moving in, and I could only guess by the gauges on the radar that it was a few hours away. "Who the hell am I supposed to notify about the warning?"

Tully grimaced and shrugged in an 'I have no clue' kind of way, just as my phone rang. I saw it was my boss and answered halfway through the first ring.

"Tell me you have good news," I said. I probably could have started with hello . . .

"I got good news and bad news," he said. "Good news is you're the temporary replacement officer. Starting today."

What?

What?

"What?!"

"I'd call it being in the right place at the right time," he said. "You get to be the boss. Isn't that what you always wanted?"

I rubbed my temple, feeling my blood pressure rise by the second. "Temporary. You said temporary. How long until they find the full-time replacement officer?"

Brian sighed. "Well, that's the bad news."

Oh no . . .

"You see, Doreen Boyle, the lady who left today? She's been waiting on a replacement for a while."

"She said she'd technically retired six months ago. Are you saying I'll be here six months?"

Tully's eyes and smile widened, excited.

"Welllllll," Brian said. "She technically applied for a replacement back in 2004."

I slow blinked.

"Two thousand and what?"

"Yeah, just don't hold your breath, Overton," Brian said. He sounded far too happy to be getting rid of me. "I sent all your employment data to HR to transfer you over to the Northern Territory bureau."

Already? He hadn't even spoken to me . . .

"I have an apartment in Melbourne, I, uh," I whispered lamely. Stupidly. My brain wasn't working.

"The bureau will cover all moving costs," he said quickly. "They'll pack your place up and send it up to you if you want."

I wasn't sure what to say.

I wasn't sure what was left to say.

"You know what you can do with my transfer papers," I said, just as the air conditioning unit began to buzz and whirr until it conked out. I stood up. "You can take the form, fold it up nicely into a neat little square." I closed my fist and punched the side of the air conditioner. It coughed back to life. "And shove it up your arse!" I disconnected the call and tossed my phone onto the instrument dash. "Argh!"

Tully stood there, wide eyed, slack-jawed but somehow grinning. "Did you just tell your boss to . . . ?"

"He's no longer my boss," I said. "Apparently I work here now." I sagged back onto the chair and held up my hand. "I think I broke it."

Laughing, Tully knelt before me and inspected my knuckles. "You have a pretty mean right hook." He gently manipulated my fingers, checking that everything still moved. "I think you'll be okay."

I nodded, fighting tears. "I'm sure everyone at the office will be pleased. They'll probably have a party in my honour right this second, to celebrate the fact I'm gone."

Tully pulled me to my feet, spun me around, and we began to do some slow, crazy waltz. He was still grinning. "No tears allowed, because this is the best day ever." I looked at him as if he'd lost his mind, and he spun me out and made me do a twirl before he pulled me back into his arms. "Now you can eat my arse and do that prostate thing all the time."

I laughed despite the emotional whirlwind and mind-fuck of the last ten minutes.

Tully pulled me flush against him, our dance now a slow sway, his eyes focused on mine. "Seriously, Jeremiah," he murmured. "I'm glad you're staying. I know this wasn't exactly what you wanted, but I think you'll love it here. If you just give it a chance." He pouted. "If you give me a chance."

I sighed. There was no way I could be mad when he was holding me like this, looking at me like that.

"I'll need to look for a place," I said. "God, I have so much to organise. I need to call my dad . . ."

My mind was beginning to swim again.

Tully held my face, grounding me. He kissed me softly. "You're stayin' with me. Take a spare room if you want. But you're still eating my arse and doing the prostate thing."

I snorted just as the radar began to beep again. That low-pressure system rolling in from the north wasn't slowing down. "There's a storm coming," I murmured.

"I know." He grinned that annoying grin that I was beginning to love. "Isn't it wonderful?"

~Fin

THE STORM BOYS SERIES

Want to read more of Tully and Jeremiah's story?

Outrun the Rain

Into the Tempest

Touch the Lightning

Or where it all began with Paul and Derek

Second Chance at First Love

THE STORM BOYS SERIES

ABOUT THE AUTHOR

N.R. Walker is an Australian author, who loves her genre of gay romance. She loves writing and spends far too much time doing it, but wouldn't have it any other way.

She is many things: a mother, a wife, a sister, a writer. She has pretty, pretty boys who live in her head, who don't let her sleep at night unless she gives them life with words.

She likes it when they do dirty, dirty things… but likes it even more when they fall in love.

She used to think having people in her head talking to her was weird, until one day she happened across other writers who told her it was normal.

She's been writing ever since…

ALSO BY N.R. WALKER

Sir

Tallowwood

Reindeer Games

The Dichotomy of Angels

Throwing Hearts

Pieces of You - Missing Pieces #1

Pieces of Me - Missing Pieces #2

Pieces of Us - Missing Pieces #3

Lacuna

Tic-Tac-Mistletoe

Bossy

Code Red

Dearest Milton James

Dearest Malachi Keogh

Christmas Wish List

Code Blue

Davo

The Kite

Learning Curve

Merry Christmas Cupid

To the Moon and Back

TITLES IN AUDIO:

Cronin's Key

Cronin's Key II

Merry Christmas Cupid

To the Moon and Back

SERIES COLLECTIONS:

Red Dirt Heart Series

Turning Point Series

Thomas Elkin Series

Spencer Cohen Series

Imago Series

Blind Faith Series

FREE READS:

Sixty Five Hours

Learning to Feel

His Grandfather's Watch (And The Story of Billy and Hale)

The Twelfth of Never (Blind Faith 3.5)

Twelve Days of Christmas (Sixty Five Hours Christmas)

Best of Both Worlds

TRANSLATED TITLES:

ITALIAN

Fiducia Cieca (Blind Faith)

Attraverso Questi Occhi (Through These Eyes)

Preso alla Sprovvista (Blindside)

Il giorno del Mai (Blind Faith 3.5)

Cuore di Terra Rossa Serie (Red Dirt Heart Series)

Natale di terra rossa (Red dirt Christmas)

Intervento di Retrofit (Elements of Retrofit)

A Chiare Linee (Clarity of Lines)

Senso D'appartenenza (Sense of Place)

Spencer Cohen Serie (including Yanni's Story)

Punto di non Ritorno (Point of No Return)

Punto di Rottura (Breaking Point)

Punto di Partenza (Starting Point)

Imago (Imago)

Imagines

Il desiderio di un soldato (A Soldier's Wish)

Scambiato (Switched)

Tallowwood

The Hate You Drink

Ho trovato te (Finders Keepers)

Cuori d'argilla (Throwing Hearts)

Galassie e Oceani (Galaxies and Oceans)

Il peso di tut (The Weight of it All)

FRENCH

Confiance Aveugle (Blind Faith)

A travers ces yeux: Confiance Aveugle 2 (Through These Eyes)

Aveugle: Confiance Aveugle 3 (Blindside)

À Jamais (Blind Faith 3.5)

Cronin's Key Series

Au Coeur de Sutton Station (Red Dirt Heart)

Partir ou rester (Red Dirt Heart 2)

Faire Face (Red Dirt Heart 3)

Trouver sa Place (Red Dirt Heart 4)

Le Poids de Sentiments (The Weight of It All)

Un Noël à la sauce Henry (A Very Henry Christmas)

Une vie à Refaire (Switched)

Evolution (Evolved)

Galaxies & Océans

Qui Trouve, Garde (Finders Keepers)

Sens Dessus Dessous (Upside Down)

La Haine au Fond du Verre (The hate You Drink)

Tallowwood

Spencer Cohen Series

GERMAN

Flammende Erde (Red Dirt Heart)

Lodernde Erde (Red Dirt Heart 2)

Sengende Erde (Red Dirt Heart 3)

Ungezähmte Erde (Red Dirt Heart 4)

Vier Pfoten und ein bisschen Zufall (Finders Keepers)

Ein Kleines bisschen Versuchung (The Weight of It All)

Ein Kleines Bisschen Fur Immer (A Very Henry Christmas)

Weil Leibe uns immer Bliebt (Switched)

Drei Herzen eine Leibe (Three's Company)

Über uns die Sterne, zwischen uns die Liebe (Galaxies and Oceans)

Unnahbares Herz (Blind Faith 1)

Sehendes Herz (Blind Faith 2)

Hoffnungsvolles Herz (Blind Faith 3)

Verträumtes Herz (Blind Faith 3.5)

Thomas Elkin: Verlangen in neuem Design

Thomas Elkin: Leidenschaft in klaren

Thomas Elkin: Vertrauen in bester Lage

Traummann töpfern leicht gemacht (Throwing Hearts)

Sir

THAI

Sixty Five Hours (Thai translation)

Finders Keepers (Thai translation)

SPANISH

Sesenta y Cinco Horas (Sixty Five Hours)

Los Doce Días de Navidad

Código Rojo (Code Red)

Código Azul (Code Blue)

Queridísimo Milton James

Queridísimo Malachi Keogh

El Peso de Todo (The Weight of it All)

Tres Muérdagos en Raya: Serie Navidad en Hartbridge

Lista De Deseos Navideños: Serie Navidad en Hartbridge

Feliz Navidad Cupido: Serie Navidad en Hartbridge

Spencer Cohen Libro Uno

Spencer Cohen Libro Dos

Spencer Cohen Libro Tres

Davo

Hasta la Luna y de Vuelta

CHINESE

Blind Faith

JAPANESE

Bossy

9 781925 886832